7/15/13
$15.00

# In the House Un-American

# IN THE
# HOUSE
# UN-AMERICAN

## BENJAMIN HOLLANDER

clockroot books

First published in 2013 by

Clockroot Books
An imprint of Interlink Publishing Group, Inc.
46 Crosby Street
Northampton, Massachusetts 01060
www.clockrootbooks.com
www.interlinkbooks.com

Library of Congress Cataloging-in-Publication Data

Hollander, Benjamin.
In the House Un-American / by Benjamin Hollander.
pages cm
ISBN 978-1-56656-927-9
1. National characteristics, American--Fiction. 2. Self-realization--Fiction.
I. Title.

PS3558.O34923I5 2013
813'.54--dc23

2013000304


Book design by Pam Fontes-May

Printed and bound in the United States of America

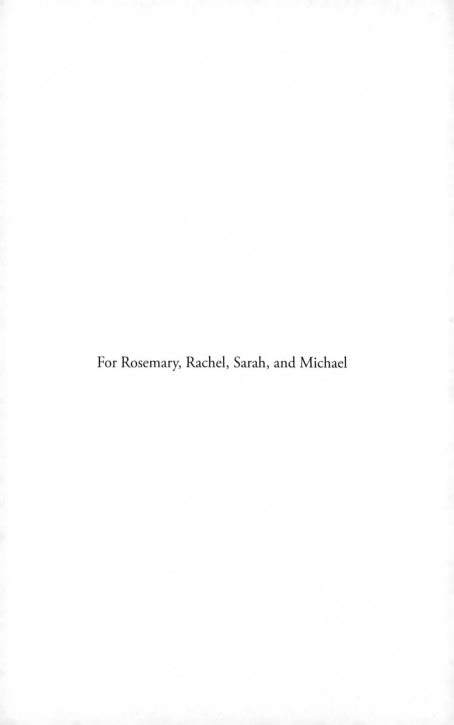

For Rosemary, Rachel, Sarah, and Michael

# CONTENTS

# 1

# Carlos Among the Fables

It was Carlos ben [בן] Carlos Rossman's mother, born when the last century turned over in the city of Leipzig, whose astonished gaze was soon steeped in an articulation about to be tripped on, as if on a wire, as she looked through the opening in the roof of his Honda, up the carved steps on the severely degreed hill into the blue sky over the far-west American city. "Those nets up in the air, there, what are they," she asked, accented, pointing to the cable car wires [sic].[1]

"Those *nets* up in the air there," captures the moments of Carlos's childhood, estranged names heard attached to objects otherwise at home in the world. This is how Carlos remembers it, the wrong and the right of a thing called into being by a name, not with a freedom to choose between names but, as Hannah once told him, as it appeared to her, with *the freedom to call something into being which did not exist before, which was not given even as an object of cognition or imagination and which therefore, strictly speaking, could not be known.* Yes, this is how Carlos remembers it, how he comes to English or, as the French would say when they translate, into the *Américain.*[2]

*

1. "Zoze nets up in ze air, zair, vat are zey" was what was really asked, in the original language, accented, pointing to the cable car wires.

2. Tr. into the "American"

Carlos ben [בן] Carlos's father had never said "in America,"
but when he grabbed Carlos by the arm—his grip tighten-
ing like a blood pressure gauge wrapped with the intent of
a smile—Carlos—and it didn't matter if he heard this as a
child, a teenager, a married man with children thinking
about his future—Carlos always knew he meant it when he
told him what's important: "What's important, is that you
be healthy and happy," his father said, years after they
landed in the mothership.

Even as a boy, Carlos had no patience with clichés, because he knew people could mean them and not mean them
at the same time. Anybody could be happy and healthy, and
anybody could not be happy and healthy.

Years after his electroshock treatment, Carlos's father
told no one how he had developed hypertension, or it could
have been years before the treatment. On the healthy happy
barometer, it didn't matter: he could be both and not both
at the same time. To be sure, no one in America would
know, since, to the bosses, he had kept the same good-
humored look now as he had then when he was given the
courtesy kick out of his job as captain of the waiters at the
Eden Hotel in Berlin in 1933, once the Nazis arrived as
guards at the voting booths, the new facts on the ground
which he saw through the hotel window and, seeing, was
soon on his way, had what they said was a way about him
which he could take around them, a smile, the same smile
Uncle Hermann once confided to him was "the chosen
vehicle of all ambiguities," to be used only if one had to
force it.

Even smiling, however, Carlos's father had never heard
the new word of "happiness" in Europe, which Hannah had

written in a letter could come only to America to be claimed like a fable, one that someone other than him and with a little more luck could have his fill of, like the future Henry Kissinger, whom he resembled but who sounded when he spoke much more content, as if he had always just finished eating: bloated, self-satisfied, sovereign, like a perched frog.

For Carlos's father, even after landing in America he could only will this "happiness" on behalf of himself with the mouth of an alien, as if it were a question, much the way the German dramatist Bertolt Brecht felt when he was quizzed by Mr. Robert Stripling, lead interrogator for the House Un-American Activities Committee in the 1940s and '50s, about the same time Carlos's father had arrived, as if he knew what it was like to come over and already be too old to be born into what's important. "To be sure," Hannah once said, in America, "among the revolutionary notions of the people themselves was happiness, that *bonheur* of which Saint-Just rightly said that it was a new word in Europe," to be rehearsed by Carlos's father every day with a smile important enough to convince his son that, yes, it *was* possible in America to appear as if he were having his fill of it.

*

In the House Un-American—so-called after a 1799 Philadelphia block of row homes deteriorated during subsequent
wars into inns for the foreign-born or lentil-soup kitchens
for the newly rumored spies or intelligence centers for the
feebleminded kind—Carlos ben [בן] Carlos and his friends—
Gingi, Berri, Mordico—were moved as children into thinking that these homes, unlike others, had taken a turn for the
worse, becoming a House Un-American—bounded by the
City's Mission Wall—inside of which the people's common
idioms turned against them one phrase at a time, slowly at
*first*, as the assimilated put up a fight but, over time, lost their
grip on things, on the good of the order, where they could
no longer command into being with a slow upturned show
of *fist* even the simplest of things, like "making a house into
a home," which, sure, would have been nice but, as it was,
turned soon enough into its Un-American other, a House
on loan where Carlos ben [בן] Carlos and friends grew up
and gathered and talked and still talk to this day about "our
Mediterranean"[3] in translation, still trying to say yes to
"American" when they come to it.

Yes, they have said yes to it for years, but they have never
acknowledged its rootedness, its by rote-ness, in the same way
people do not face the lie in the song at their fingertips, the
lie they overlook when they overhear the song and follow it,
as if someone were whistling them into the memory of their
first love, together alone. They say yes to it. How could they
not? How else, when they think back, could that ancient
song, *under the boardwalk*, have the effect it does if not by
turning the Coney Island Atlantic Ocean into the sea, only
so that the lying rime could keep love alive, "down by the sea
/ on a blanket with my baby / is where I'll be," where else, as

if it were "our Mediterranean"[3] in translation they found there, when they came to it as young drifters to America.

"But the truth is, there is no one America or American," one of Carlos ben [בן] Carlos's friends will declare, when pressed, in order to distinguish himself from the others. "America, you know, is not so simple, you can't reduce it to an American type you say yes or no to, like this or that earnest intonation—it's a big country, you know, and these people have differences, not to mention regions and religions," he says. "In these times, and with all the diverse, it's hard to claim only *one* kind of this species of American. Everyone is welcome."

Here, of course, he sounds like Rezi, the poet Carlo Rezi, from that now unremembered poem of the '30s, comforting the frustrated woman talking trash about the illegals on the bus—"why don't they talk American," she says—and Rezi says:

> You must not be so impatient…
> English is not an easy language to learn.
> Besides, if they don't learn it, their children will:
> We have good schools, you know.

Yes, be patient. Everyone is welcome. Or will be.

Of course, on one level the others know this but are not convinced—they even suspect Rezi's response is a bit too well meaning, the "there-there my dear" manner of intonation a bit too English, an eloquence in question to begin with, a bit cracked to be truly American. So they wonder: if everyone is truly welcome, why does there exist, in phrase and condition, the un-American—"my father," so Carlos

once overheard, "never felt American" yet could never pin-
point what it would have felt to be one. He felt, the phrase
was, "un-American," a condition that transcended politics.
He never went to high school or lived in England, so where—
the question was overheard—as a Jew hiding in plain sight
on a German cargo ship traversing the Mediterranean Levant
in the 1930s as a cook's apprentice—the potato stoker, they
called him, because he was always sweating and turning over
potatoes, *Hier Heisse Essen,* "eat hot here," read the chalked
sign hung in the bowels of the ship, translated by the crew as
*Heisse Scheisse Hier,* "get your hot shit here" in steerage, from
port to port over five years Carlos's father picked up as they
all did the random six languages needed to declare refugee
status outside their right to any state—legal freaks, Hannah
called them, for whom committing a crime was the only way
to get their day in court, to eat, be bedded, be doctored in a
nation-state which passed their kind over for asylum to be
among the un-born human, the un-persons

—so where—the question was overheard—did Carlos's father, already an un-person, pick up a tone outside his station when he arrived in America using his voice, a bulge in his throat, exposed, that would take on the mark of Cain to the New Men in the New Land who saw or heard him, like a ventriloquist missing his dummy, six languages hiding in plain sight in his throat and fronted by a cosmopolitan English among Americans who he heard were as at home in their own skins as they were suspect of the languages he brought with him. So he lived between false options: as a worker among workers speaking outside his class, or as the quiet American hiding the languages he knew they distrusted, since they insinuated, in phrase or condition, heard or un-heard, "the un-American," the un-welcomed: the potato stoker from steerage who had stepped out of his apron and slipped into a black tux as captain of the waiters center stage under the arched spotlights illuminating the natural theater of the Oak Room in New York's Plaza Hotel. *One could scarcely imagine human figures in that room, so royal did it look*, heraldic emblems and medals and murals of castle miniatures set to disappear in the wash of light against the walls, with Carlos's father soon to use the same smile Uncle Hermann told him was "the chosen vehicle of all ambiguities" as a *rapprochement* with these patrons of America for whom the best he could do to mimic their Order of Confidence was to prematurely step in and bribe them into his space, saying: "Good evening, gentlemen, may I offer you *the usual* from the bar?"

Who, then, would this un-American father be up
against, if not only *one* kind of this species of American confidence, since it would be an uphill battle at the very least
to maintain being an un-American up against *all* kinds of
species of American, particularly welcoming, diverse ones?
Carlos only wished his father had felt this welcomed, but it
wasn't happening.

By and by, unlike Carlos ben [בן] Carlos's father, the
friends have tried to welcome themselves. Although they
have been trying to say yes to "American" for years, when
they talk about "Our Mediterranean" in translation, about
where they come from, the translation into American English is almost invisible, since no one in Carlos ben [בן] Carlos's circle even knows he is speaking outside his mother
tongue. The translation and the idea of translation inhabit

the three of them, who have been invited to come to this Writer's House in the city of Philadelphia, and one of them, now in Philly, asks himself—it will be the subject of his talk—outside the box but not quizzically:

"How did I come to English?"

Back home, before he leaves for Philly, a friend says, *she says it like a teacher*, and quizzically:

"In America, what you say sounds strange. The fact is: no one here *comes* to English. No one says it like that, as if you were coming to, say, Philadelphia. Yes, if you want to, you can come to Philly, but not to English."

"But a language is like a city, no?" he says, trying to make the case in good form before he leaves her house.

"Interesting metaphor, yes, but no, one does not come to it. Anyway, it really doesn't matter, you're not fooling anyone here, since otherwise you sound as if you've already arrived."

\*

That's the problem, Carlos thinks. When we talk about "our Mediterranean" in translation, we sound fluent, as if we've already arrived as Americans in Philly. No doubt, with our English as good as it is and our papers in order, everyone will welcome us as Americans, so why protest their invitation. If we sound fluency, and we write poetry which appears to articulate that condition—*Carlos thinks hard about this*—a reader will not acknowledge wires as nets in a poem as anything but metaphor for the mill. What Yves Bonnefoy says about the German-language poet Paul Celan's anguish in Paris when he was charged with plagiarism by Ivan Goll's wife, Claire, first in 1949 and then in 1960, applies here as it did there. It was not plagiarism as plagiarism that was the problem then, but the attack against the urgent singularity of significance in Celan's *polis*, which encompassed the loss of his parents in the Holocaust as well as his own trials in a Nazi labor camp. How could anyone believe, Celan appears to have thought, that he could have substituted or weighted his poems with words outside his particular life—in Paris, where he ultimately settled, in exile from his home and a German language turned barbarian—and let them appear the same in his poems as they had appeared in Goll's? Similarly, how could anyone believe those nets *behaved* as metaphor rather than knowing that Carlos *der Jüngere, the younger one among the fables born from the facts on the ground,* was getting it called wrong yet again.

*

In 1969, because of the overwhelming fact of it, and his still being like a newcomer to the language he'd adopted ten years earlier, no one around him noticed the presence of this odd, three-folded name or, if they did, no one told Berri about it. The fact was: "Berri" was the Leipzig mother's German-inflected English shout-out transliteration of the Hebrew *Ber-El* [באר אל], the well of G-D, transmuted into an elongated *Berri* each time she high-pitch cried it with a follow-up whistling from their fourth-floor tenement window to the playground where he was among his friends, as embarrassed an un-American sounding as could be, *Berri,* unlike the common bass-toned "Barry" his friends turned it into being, "a kid called Barry," just like any other American with an Irish lilt and gait, which he wasn't, at the time, nor could imagine ever being, in 1969, like any other Barry in this America's future:

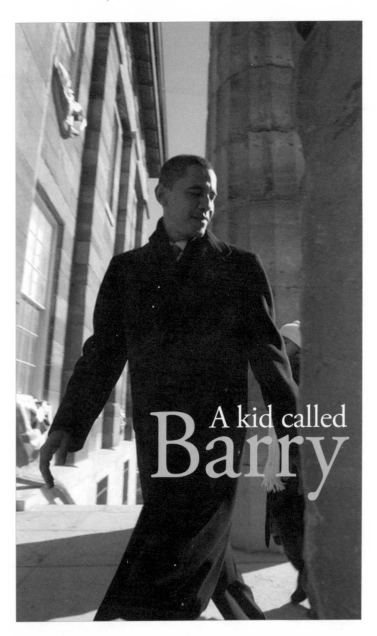

A kid called Barry

He thought: if one was called by three names in sequence, one could be as old an American type as a man on a wanted poster hung in a far western post office of the country, a Civil War soldier, or a young aristocrat on its eastern coast. Anyone in America could be John Wayne Gacy.*

Or Barack Hussein Obama.

Three names in sequence spelled an American genre.

Or two names, side by side, first name as last name, last name as first name, spelled an America in which one could be one and the other, it just made common sense, he thought, like a reversible raincoat, to be both "I say what I mean and I mean what I say," as if one's name was called into being under the unprecedented conditions of equality and never put into question, each name, like the person it was bound to be, allowed to mind its own business, free to be first or last, for the Left or for the Right, to claim the right to keep and bear pot or arms, arms for pot, pot for arms, it didn't matter which, it was a matter of honor to protect either one or the other, as good as one's word to keep, free to fire and smoke at the same time, to say "I say what I mean and I mean what I say," or "Ah, let 'em weep," which was just to say…

Anyone in America could be Ron Paul.**

So when his teachers claimed Berri was just right in English and thus in his head from the moment he said "yes" in it at the age of six after arriving at the harbor of the New-York of the New Land, he seized a particular kind of

* 1970s American serial killer and leader of his township's Democratic Party.
** Ronald Ernest "Ron" Paul (born August 20, 1935), American congressman and presidential candidate for the Libertarian Party in 1988, and again for the Republican Party in 2008 and in 2012.

invisible ownership of the language—somewhat like Xerox did with the copy, advertising itself out behind the scenes in the land of plenty—an ironic kind of Americanness he never felt but projected, without anyone noticing what of this language belonged to who of his person, as silent and screened, at the time, as the name "Carlos" in the iconic three-folded name of the American poet William Carlos Williams—who today would be framed as the white American male poet William Carlos Williams.

Strange. At the time, no one knew or even asked about this Carlos, who or why his middle name was Carlos, his name later discovered to have come into being after the brother of his Puerto Rican mother, yet who knew, at the time, of a Puerto Rican mother at the heart of this white American poet's calling, certainly not Carlos ben [בן] Carlos Rossman or his friend Berri, for example, naturalized Americans in Queens, both of whose mothers were born in the city of Leipzig, Germany, at the turn of the last century, although their families went deeper in time into the Eastern past, into what was then called Posen, the future Poland, which they had left Leipzig for just before the war to escape the Nazis—*you know who they are*, the mothers used to whisper to their children in America about anyone they thought was either following them or going the other way, it didn't matter, if they thought they looked like Nazis, *you know who they are,* they whispered to their children, who were born after the war and who had never known any Nazis. A mistake, in hindsight, more menacing, to be sure, to be invisible, a rumor, for the children to have never known Nazis yet live with them as if their names and faces were just coming into being in their bedroom closets, to be sure, the family could escape quietly to Warsaw because they thought it was safer than Leipzig, so that they went there not to be shot in the ghetto but the Nazis followed them into the future, at least this is what was rumored, what they told their children, but Carlos and Berri, naturalized Americans in Queens, got to wondering why an American poet would say he wanted his poems to sound an authentic American speech, the same as that which could, he emphasized, *come out of the mouths of Polish mothers*, which would have been fine by Carlos and Berri, though a bit curious, to be sure, since they wondered, looking back, why could he not have made the speech coming out of these mothers' mouths his own, Puerto Rican. The fact that he didn't threw them.

So, *it was*, Carlos and Xerox, passing…

This is just to say: on 85th Road, in Queens among the Puerto Ricans, Berri remembered, no one had heard of this Carlos, poet, strangely bookended by the same plain name, William Williams.

Or of his grandmother: Emily Dickenson Wellcome.

*

Among William Williams and the Puerto Ricans, Carlos talked to Dennis about Dennis's father, who was a 1950s American hydraulic engineer and needed to know that when you worked, you produced. He had no truck with the nation of counterfeiters and confidence men who waited for you to buy into a promise, speculators who had shaped one vision of the history of the republic in what Uncle Hermann had called "the Wall Street Spirit." He would barter if he thought what you offered him reflected the value of what he offered you. Dennis's parents ran a dry-goods store—textiles and buttons and hats—which Carlos heard as a "dried goods store," imagining a surplus of old raisins and apricots, sacks of flour, not knowing what this kind of store stood for in an American's *Weltanschauung*. His father, Dennis said, learned early: if there was a wheelbarrow in the yard, in the back of the store, and he could go a day without moving supplies in it, he would exchange it for an offer of a chicken, if the offer of a chicken came his way and if, of course, he needed the eggs for his family. "Would he," Carlos asked Dennis, "accept a poem?"

"Well, he did not read much of poetry, but when he did he could get to like it," his son told Carlos.

"So what if I walked in with a copy of William Carlos Williams's poem 'The Red Wheelbarrow,' which begins

so much depends
upon

a red wheel
barrow

"Well," the son said, "it depends. If it was the poem William Carlos Williams had written, he'd take it, but not if you signed off on it."

*

Carlos ben [בן] Carlos overheard:

*like any outsider, you cope, you try to copy to belong, you overcompensate for what you think you hear is the norm.*

He did not hear these exact words—they were too complex, too big for a child laborer squatting in the corner of the Mission Wall.

But not hearing them did not stop him. He tried to write what he overheard: *be clear, be specific, be precise.*

*Up Against the Wall.*

\*

The boy has a choice: keep silent or run on. One version, the first one, has him being the quiet American, but Carlos can't assume this act.

So he assumes the other—so he writes and writes and thinks he's going native.

*be clear, be specific, be precise.*

"Clear, concise, correct, that's my motto," says Bob Sheppard, NY Yankees stadium announcer. But who, you wonder, is Bob Sheppard, NY Yankees stadium announcer. A dominant species of American?

*Remember*, Carlos the laborer thinks and shines his shoes, *The American is explicit but level. Like his confidence. Literally: a word he uses and uses. And believes is true. Really. And believes himself fair. From afar. You may hear him talking evenly, openly—like an engineer, about Jesus.*

\*

"We get it," Carlos overhears. The voice is a flat, impatient twang, the pronunciation of an American poet. "We get it," the American poet says, "don't intellectualize it, *if you get the gasworks into a poem, you've got America, boy*. Get it?"

Carlos does not get it. To get the gasworks into a poem is too explicit, to copy his namesake Carlos, the poet W.W., *would be to get as much into the composition as he can in the fewest possible words, trimming whatever wherever it is possible to make the sense come through without tautology*, but it would be too explicit for this Carlos, which is why he can't do it, which is why, when he wants to be explicit, he goes round and round in his writing like any good ESL boy and overcompensates in order to be clear, specific, precise, why use one word where two will do, to over-hit the mark to get to the target, imagine the tabula rasa—page, screen, wall, whatever—as a dartboard in a dive bar and the words as darts in each black wedge leading to the bull's-eye, the point, and now the guys are drunk and the board starts spinning and Carlos wants to hit each wedge to make a point, to make it again, because each wedge on its own but from a distinct angle will extend down towards the bull's-eye, round and round to get to the point because he wants to leave nothing out, unexplained, if this sounds like bull-shit so be it but it's not, it's just like Carlos, illegal, not like his namesake, the poet W.W., to come into the place, to be pal-o-mining it up with the guys, his own way to tell a story, a joke, listen, he says, a guy walks into a bar, eventually.

\*

Carlos dreams another Carlos, the poet, speaking of his dominant species of American, like Mencken's: "Here lies the secret, in the monotony of our intonation, of much that we might tell."

But what is there to tell? The sound of the facts? Eugen, *Carlos remembers and shines his shoes*, says the sound of *the axe* is the natural philosophy of America, a land of bosses, but Carlos hears Eugen saying the sound of *the facts* is the natural philosophy of America, the bosses of facts, overheard, evenly intoning a culture of evidence, if not on this day for the bottom line then on the next day for the miracles of Jesus' time.

*

At 13, when the boy wanted to be the son of no one—certainly not a bookended Xerox of Carlos—he became Carlos Kiner Rossman, the boy from New Mexico who would be the man out of this corner of New York, *Kiner's Korner.*

*Kiner's Korner*, of course, was a television show, which is why Carlos chose it, the home of Ralph Kiner, the boy from New Mexico, former left fielder for the Pirates of Pittsburgh, yet who knew what city belonged to this person, who once called himself Ralph Korner, certainly not Carlos, for whom the old man played either in a newsreel before he was born, or it was before he became a citizen that Carlos ben [בן] Carlos heard that voice who interviewed the Amazin' Mets of '69, the twang in his name, *Kiner*, his called fly ball a *can-o-kern* in the microphone, which Carlos overheard and absorbed into his mock calls from home, "*Carlos Raalph Keeyner here,*" and which said America as much as it said "no one" to a boy in a nation he would only later find out was deaf to the import of translation.

*

# 2

# Beyond Carlos: An American Interrogation

Beyond Carlos ben [בן] Carlos, beyond Carlos Kiner Ross-man, beyond Berri and Gingi and Mordico, I like to use myself as a species of un-American, an example of the kind sounded in poetry, ESL inscribed within ESL, English as a Second Language confronted by English as a Sovereign Language, but with a difference.

Unlike the immigrant I was, or even the child of an immigrant I was, which I can claim I am like Amy Tan, I don't want you to think about the particulars of my identity, about my deferential second-language status, about my inspirational difference from others to which every immigrant is welcome as a subject—so is America represented as a nation of inspirational difference-from-others-stories to which everyone is welcome as a subject—since who are you when I do claim this but someone who is obliged to relate, to be inspired, to be different like me, only different. I want you to be more than that. It is only the blind groping weirdness I want to relate. And the stuff of poetry: everyone is not welcome. That's the difference.

It's not that I am of the kind—that species of un-American—who has English as a Second Language, even as, yes, I do, and can at the same time say yes to American. Or that I can distinguish like Amy Tan the distinct Englishes which appear in my novels—she goes on in the clear essay about how her mother's "broken" English among other Englishes has informed her writing. That is very much something a teacher of English can do, and can only apply to its appearance in my novels.

The fact is: I have no novels, and I don't remember English as anything but my first language even as it unclearly was not, so that it's a matter of hearing it as a second language only within *my feeling*—this oceanic feeling one can absorb, in fact, through a conch shell—that it was anything but my first, which is crucial and the stuff of poetry.

If you care, poetry, I have overheard, comes like this kind of underwater English to one who speaks like this, because poetry is already the sounding of a second language within an American culture that does not count it among its facts, its culture of evidence, and, in my case, it becomes a triple threat, the ESL boy—not to be pitied like iron-lung boy—who falls in love with poetry as a second language cadence which must always resist English as a sovereign language cadence, even as the boy must live and breathe it within its nation, as his mother sounds it otherwise, as if he will never have arrived. It's the matter and the mother of hearing all this I am after.

This is why I want you to hear Parnell Thomas or Robert E. Stripling, interrogators of the German dramatist Bertolt Brecht and the composer Hanns Eisler—Leipzig-born and brother of Gerhart Eisler, whom the committee was really after since he was, according to his sister, who testified against him before the committee, "a leading agent of the Russian police," she said, "a most dangerous terrorist," she said, "the perfect terrorist type," she said, a breeder of future al-Qaeda secret cells and watchwords—when they appeared separately in 1947 before the House Un-American

Activities Committee investigating so-called communists among us, before you were born, to expose "that secret monotony of our intonation" of which Carlos said "there is much to tell." In the tone of this dominant species of American, I want you to hear words spoken as if they had no right to exist but much to tell. Perhaps other languages have this tone, but I only hear it in this one:

MR. STRIPLING: Now Mr. Brecht, what is your occupation?

MR. BRECHT: I am a poet and a playwright.

MR. STRIPLING: A poet and a playwright?

MR. BRECHT: Yes.

MR. STRIPLING: Where are you presently employed?

MR. BRECHT: I am not employed.

There is much to tell in Stripling's "a poet and playwright?"— as if these words had no right to exist, specifically in America. In America, in fact, Stripling's words sound alien before they can even represent aliens, before, that is, they represent poet and playwright humans not fit to be employed and, therefore, who look quizzical just standing around. This is what the un-American feels, his condition, if you care, is that he appears to others like a poem, quizzical, without much use, just standing around. It makes one wonder why in the drama of Brecht and Eisler's forced testimony in front of the Un-American Committee, the witnesses' brief focus on the American poem and the fate of poetry in translation goes rarely mentioned. Given the specter of deportation on the grounds of their alliances with the Communist Party in any country, as the lead chairman put it, it's no wonder that any commentary on poetry and translation would sink under the radar. (To think, if this were my testimony, that these words could come back to haunt me, is to realize how un-American they might appear since no one says it like that here, as Carlos's friend once said. For sure, any commentary on poetry might "pass" or "slide under the radar" but it would never "sink," or it would only sink if somehow, like a submarine, no one saw it coming...) Yet it is exactly their testimony on poetry and translation which is a window into the house of the un-American, as if it were *The House on 92nd Street*, a 1945 semi-documentary noir film about American Nazis recruited by Germans in America. Curiously, this is also about the time that the U.S. government's Operation Paperclip is in full throttle, recruiting German Nazi scientists, doctors, engineers, and so on into the American technological war against the Soviet Union. Historically, what we're caught in here is a VISE—a Virtual Intelligence School Exchange program—you give me your Nazi experimental science guys—*you know who they are*—and we'll give you and the world our Hollywood propaganda films with just the facts of our stentorian narrators.

At the time, one could agree or argue with the role of the Un-American Committee in determining political alliances or questioning who among the native-born or naturalized among us was or was not a patriot, just as today FBI counter-terrorism media consultant man Brad Garrett can warn us about the thoughts of a Muslim citizen of

America who, himself, may not be capable of being a threat to the country but, with those "bad thoughts," may be drawn to "the bad guys"—Brad's words—who are not citizens but bomb-capable, which is why we have to be in a state of vigilance towards the un-American American's "bad thoughts"—Brad's words—which back in the day, a little history tells us, belonged to the communists among us and, if we go further back in the day, well… it's bad. This is only to say that, politically, one can determine who belongs to the un-American camp at any time, and that is your opinion, and on that opinion the accused lose jobs and reputations for life. No small thing. But the point is, even these so-called Un-Americans look *deeply American*—at least one dominant species of deeply American—next to Mr. Brecht and Mr. Eisler, so that, concerning Mr. Brecht and Mr. Eisler, the committee got their un-American *camp* right, although they had no clue what it was, as they got right in the face of the timidly appeasing appearances of Mr. Brecht, for whom translation is a ruse, yes, but a ruse with integrity. Why else, with his English as good as it is, does he accept the chairman's friendly offer of a translator as if the chairman were saying, "please, Mr. Brecht, have another smoke," with Brecht's cigar in full view, "Yes, thank you, I wouldn't mind having another at the ready," Mr. Brecht says, as if Mac the Knife were appearing as Wally Cox in the voice of Mr. Peepers—and the chairman, of course, square-jawed, earnest, stentorian, starts asking questions within the culture of evidence he knows, one that demands he have confidence in the questions' abilities to answer themselves:

**Mr. Stripling:** Have you ever, Mr. Brecht, made application to the Communist Party?

I would like to ask Mr. Brecht whether or not he wrote a poem, a song, entitled "Forward, We've Not Forgotten?"

And, Mr. Brecht, did you not collaborate with Hanns Eisler on the song "In Praise of Learning"? Now I will read you the words and ask you if this is the one:

> *Learn now the simple truth, you for whom the time has come at last; it is not too late.*
> *Learn now the ABC. It is not enough but learn it still Fear not, be not downhearted. You must learn the lesson, you must be ready to take over.*

**Mr. Brecht:** No, excuse me, that is the wrong translation. That is not right. (*Laughter.*) Just one second, and I will give you the correct text.

**Mr. Stripling:** That is not a correct translation?

**Mr. Brecht:** That is not correct, no; that is not the meaning. It is not very beautiful, but I am not speaking about that.

**Mr. Stripling:** What does it mean? I have here a portion of *The People*, which was issued by the Communist Party of the United States… Page 24 says: In Praise of Learning, by Bert Brecht; music by Hanns Eisler. It says here:

> *You must be ready to take over; learn it.*
> *Men on the dole, learn it; men in the prisons, learn it, women in the kitchen, learn it; men of 65, learn it.*
> *You must be ready to take over.*

**Mr. Brecht:** Mr. Stripling, maybe his translation—

**The Translator (Mr. Baumgardt):** The correct translation would be, "You must take the lead."

**The Chairman:** "You must take the lead"?

**The Translator:** "The lead." It definitely says "The lead." It is not "You must take over." The translation is not a literal translation of the German.

**Mr. Stripling:** Well, Mr. Brecht, as it has been published in these publications of the Communist Party, then, if that is incorrect, what did you mean?

**Mr. Brecht:** I don't remember never—I never got that book myself. I must not have been in the country when it was published. I think it was published as a song, one of the songs Eisler had written the music to. I did not give any permission to publish it. I don't see—I think I never saw the translation.

**Mr. Stripling:** Do you have the words there before you?

**Mr. Brecht:** In German, yes.

**Mr. Stripling:** Of the song?

**Mr. Brecht:** Oh yes; in the book.

**Mr. Stripling:** Not in the original.

**Mr. Brecht:** In the German book…

**Mr. Stripling:** Did you ever, Mr. Brecht, make application to join the Communist Party?

**Mr. Brecht:** I do not understand the question. Did I make—

**Mr. Stripling:** Have you ever made application to join the Communist Party?

**Mr. Brecht:** No, no, no, no, no, never.

But who takes the lead here between interrogator and witness? Who is spinning? Who is leading whom? "I don't remember never... I think I never saw the translation," Mr. Brecht says. This is how he takes the lead, how he never answers by thinking, as if this dialogue is a dance and things start spinning away. Everyone is at a remove. The un-American lives at a remove, with leading answers to leading questions. He removes himself, he is alienated before Mr. Stripling, stripping the hearing of its self-evident character, and Mr. Brecht becomes that little alien man, you know, "you are a curious little man, Herr Brecht," at a remove, as Mr. Brecht is from the House Committee, as the translator is from Mr. Brecht, as Mr. Brecht is from his collaborator, Hanns Eisler, and is further from Eisler's brother, whom the committee is really after when they go for Mr. Brecht, who spins them into airing his views on translation and his misunderstanding of politics when they want their questions, answered, their facts on the ground. "I am certain," he says, "I think I never saw the translation," he says, and removes himself. Mr. Stripling and the chairman insist he stay:

**Mr. Stripling:** Mr. Brecht, since you have been in the United States, have you attended any Communist Party meetings? [**Leading the witness, assuming he knows what Communist Party meetings are**]

MR. BRECHT [**sounding quizzical**]: No, I don't think so.

MR. STRIPLING: You don't think so?

MR. BRECHT: No.

THE CHAIRMAN: Well, aren't you certain?

MR. BRECHT: No—I am certain; yes.

THE CHAIRMAN: You are certain you have never been to Communist Party meetings?

MR. BRECHT: Yes; I think so. I am here 6 years—I am here those—I do not think so. I do not think that I attended political meetings. [**Leading the interrogator by assuming Communist Party meetings are "political," sounding as if he does not know if they are or are not.**]

THE CHAIRMAN: No; never mind the political meetings, but have you attended any Communist meetings in the United States?

MR. BRECHT: I do not think so; no. [**Well, of course, if they are not political, then it is as if he has not attended them. That settles that.**]

THE CHAIRMAN: You are certain?

MR. BRECHT: I think I am certain.

THE CHAIRMAN: You think you are certain?

MR. BRECHT: Yes, I have not attended such meetings, in my opinion.

As he is entitled to in America, Mr. Brecht, as Hannah once told him it appeared to her, states his opinion. "Yes, I have not attended such meetings, in my opinion." In fact, and strangely maybe only in America is this possible, he turns the fact of his non-attendance at Communist Party meetings *into an opinion*, as if he were standing in for another's view, perhaps at one remove from what actually happened, which he remembers having once been told is the true significance of having, in the ancient Greek *polis*, an opinion, not in order to understand another's view but to stand in for it, perhaps like the United States itself, being only an opinion, only standing in for the republic it used to be.

But who knows? The committee seems satisfied that he is trying hard to answer the questions, and that's all that matters, even if Mr. Brecht keeps himself from the certainty of the facts, which he can do only in America by stating his opinion. Where else can a fact be accepted as an opinion except in a country that keeps faith in the facts, to which everyone is welcome.

But who knows what really happened? Did he attend meetings? Did he collaborate with Eisler's brother? Are the songs rallying cries to take over the hearts of the American people? Obviously, the committee seems satisfied with his answers, most likely because he has established himself as a good boy, an innocent: how could he possibly have known of let alone attended Communist Party meetings if he never attended, as he says, political meetings. In fact, in Brecht's facts, he may not even have known what Communist Party meetings might be, as if they're a bit quizzical, as he says, like Mac the Knife being Wally Cox in the Bavarian voice of Mr. Peepers: "I *sink* I am certain I never attended," like a good boy. Even the committee thinks so: "Mr. Brecht, you are a good example to the other witnesses," a statement Bert did not take to. "What do they mean, I'm a good example. Let me tell you something," he once told his friend Eric, a year after he sat in the House Caucus Room: "The Americans were witch-hunters, true, but they were polite and sincere," Bert said, "as if everyone was welcome to the hearing. They even let me smoke my cigar in the room. I could never have smoked my cigar in front of the Nazis, but in America anything was possible, as long as you got straight to the point. So, when they were questioning me, I smoked it, I tapped it, I jerked it, and no doubt it was seen in silhouette, like a hand puppet shadowing a wall in front of the cameras. I used it to manufacture pauses with between their questions and my answers. No doubt, in Germany, they would have never let me act like that, and I would have been arrested before I took the first puff. That's why I say in America, with the right cigar, anything is possible."

And everyone *is* welcome, except, perhaps, for Bert's friend Hanns Eisler.

Accused of being the brother of Gerhart Eisler, "the terrorist type," he says: "Does the committee believe that brotherly love is un-American? The committee hopes that by persecuting me it will intimidate many other artists in America whom it may dislike for any of various unworthy reasons…. It is horrible to think what will become of American art if this committee is to judge what art is American and what is un-American…. This is the sort of thing Hitler and Mussolini tried. They were not successful, and neither will be the House Committee on Un-American Activities."

Perhaps. But the fact is Eisler *does* judge, does distinguish between American poetry and German poetry, when he addresses the committee about his work, the words "between those sheets of music," which they ridicule:

**MR. McDowell (FROM THE COMMITTEE):** I think all members of the committee should examine these exhibits, which ridicule the law, which oppose the prohibitions of abortions, which could not be sent through the U.S. mail. I don't know what the custom is in Germany or Austria, but such words as are between those sheets of music have no place in any civilization.

**MR. EISLER:** They are considered great poetry.

**MR. McDowell:** They are considered as what?

**MR. EISLER:** Great poetry.

**MR. McDowell:** Well, great poetry as we are taught in America has nothing to do with that kind of truck.

**MR. RANKIN:** I am conscious when I look at this filth here—

**MR. EISLER:** Excuse me—it is not filth. May I ask you: how are you familiar with American poetry?

**MR. RANKIN:** American what?

**MR. EISLER:** Poetry.

**MR. RANKIN:** Poetry.

**MR. EISLER:** And American writing. This is not American poetry or writing. This was written in German. It is not translated. It was written in Berlin in 1927. I say again it is great poetry. We can have different tastes in art, but I can't permit that you call my work in such names.

**MR. RANKIN:** I suppose that I am as familiar with American poetry and with English poetry generally as any member of the House. And anybody that tries to tell me that this filth is poetry certainly reads himself out of the class of any American poet that has ever been recognized by the American people.


Mr. Rankin and Mr. Eisler: they look at each other and talk about the American poem and the fate of German poetry in translation, about the American and the un-American. Mr. Eisler is a stranger to this House, an un-person, an un-person who wants to infiltrate the House with great poetry, with the roundness of German poetry vs. its American translation. But Mr. Rankin is rankled—he wants the facts while he offers opinions. He wants them in earnest, with a sincerity that is stubborn, stentorian. This is how facts are performed in the House, in public, with a sincerity and confidence that is stubborn, why the straight-talking Wyoming senator Alan Simpson, years later, can be admired when he demands that it is "time now for the facts. In America, everyone is entitled to their own opinions, but no one is entitled to their own facts," as if adopting and ascribing an aristocratic neutrality to the facts in order to justify their conviction, like Mr. Rankin, when he faces this stranger, the un-person, and references "poetry" as this fabled thing outside the facts he knows, this fabled quizzical thing which the un-person asks Mr. Rankin if he knows:

**MR. EISLER:** May I ask you: how are you familiar with American poetry?

**MR. RANKIN:** [**in the hard-of-hearing dismissive tone**] American what?

**MR. EISLER:** [**in the full, round seductive tone**] Poetry.

**MR. RANKIN:** [**flatly with disdain**] Poetry.

With a disdain for the Germans' poetry, for the witnesses who speak of its alien presence, Mr. Rankin seems rankled by the fact of it. He resembles Mr. Brecht's Mr. Keuner in his *Stories of Mr. Keuner*, who said: "I, too, once adopted an aristocratic stance (you know: erect, upright, and proud, head thrown back). I was standing in rising water at the time. I adopted this stance when it rose to my chin."

For this committee and its nation, one could only wonder when the time would come for an un-person's poetry to take its revenge and flow through the House like floodwater.[3]

3. Our Mediterranean

# 3

# Our Mediterranean

**First Fact:**
**Say Yes to American:**

**BERRI**: Gingi, just between us, our nicknames, but you first, yes?

**GINGI**: Yes, my Mediterranean began on the Atlantic Coast, first frontier of the new world, in a fishing village called Gloucester settled by Portuguese immigrants.

**BERRI**: Yes, my Mediterranean began on the Middle Eastern coast of Haifa, Israel, which I left when I was six for New York, "first frontier of the new world." And you, Mordico?

**MORDICO**: Yes, in 1959 I left the hurly-burly of Turkey, its rich vein of bigotry and psychic resonance, behind. Though I did not focus on it then, I left my mother tongue behind, which is Turkish, which I am not. In 1961 I decided to become a writer. As an American writer my first act was self-immolation. I had to destroy the Turkishness in me, feel, hopefully, one day, dream in English. If I had thought in Turkish, I aborted it, nicked it. I chose not to have a thought exist unless originating in English, a language which overwhelmed me because I had said my first words in it only six years before.

**GINGI**: I was in love with words. Although I expressed my identity in a way that was polemically American, embracing the poetics of William Carlos Williams and his contempt for T.S. Eliot and anything continental, I still longed for the meaning that a color could have in Lorca, for the "red earth" of Pavese. My access to those texts came partly from my parents' "secret" language, the Italian they had acquired as immigrants in their flight from Yugoslavia, and the fifteenth-century Spanish that filtered down to me from an older generation. Although my family seemed "European," something was different: my name told me as much. After all, the first name was Hebrew and the last name Arabic and both languages were very far from any standard curriculum.

**BERRI**: "Yes," I remember my first word in American English was "yes," and I remember as a boy speaking quickly, effortlessly, without a trace of an accent in American English. And, just as swiftly, I remember losing my Hebrew vocabulary, as my parents spoke German at home, which I understood but never spoke. As a child I said "no" to both. Today the question is this: how does the loss of one (Hebrew) vocabulary and the resistance to another (German) enter with an accent into my writing? Or put another way: in America, how was saying "no" to these languages secretly betrayed over time by the poetry I wrote in the American English, which, yes, said "yes," but with an untraceable accent.

**MORDICO**: Now, as a thinking adult in English, I speak it with an accent. I speak Turkish also with an accent. Turkish is an unaccented, flat language, with vowels of equal length. The accentual rhythms of English interfere with my Turkish. When I speak, Turks think I am a Cypriot or Armenian, an outsider. I must spend weeks in Turkey, speaking no English, for my accent in Turkish almost to disappear. My business is antique Oriental rugs, which is dominated by Persian Jews. My Persian has improved incredibly. I can speak the daily business lingo, its bargainings, lies, theatrics, jokes (at which I am very good) without effort; but I am illiterate in Persian. Occasionally, one of the merchants, knowing I am also a poet, recites a Sadi or Hafiz poem, which is completely incomprehensible (and slightly repulsive) to me... Not only do I speak English, but also, mentally, in my mind's eye, hear it with an accent. The true power, even nature of American for me is accented, buried in this accent... The true power of language, its well of inspiration, for me, lie in its conscious or unconscious errors, cracks, imperfections. I am a poet, an American poet, because I have a defective ear. And, first lesson: this defect is the source of my possible talents and their limitations.

**GINGI:** This insistence on discovering the wound in every word carries with it the effort to democratize language. No?

**BERRI:** Yes, I speak for myself when to speak of an "un-American poetry" for a poet writing in English but whose English is accented or a bit cracked in its fluency, is exactly this and more: to not only discover "the wound in every word in the effort to democratize language," but to uncover the world in the wound exposed—in English. No?

**MORDICO:** Yes, to speak of an "un-American poetry" is to be anti-modern, searching for an essence, not in words but among words—to help English grow a limb it does not have.

(Mordico adds:)

> *(i realize. some of us never spawned street names.*
> *i realize. some of us never spawned nick names.)*
>
> *(from SOULJAM*
> *by Küçük Iskender*
> *translated by Murat Nemet-Nejat)*

# 4

# Hearings in Progress

First Testimony
(On Progress)

Sixty years had passed since the Judges and the Witness gazed at each other in the committee room under the mural signed "America at Peace." Today, their roles would be reversed. Carlos would hear the difference in their tone, in our twenty-first-century time:

Judge: *You speak of the un-American as a kind—in poetry, in manner, in feeling, in thought.*

Witness: *Yes.*

Judge: *You can't.*

Witness: *Why?*

Judge: *The American won't let you.*

Witness: *Which American?*

Judge: *That's right.*

## Second Testimony

If every other country had its genetic-cultural markers, Carlos thought, why were Americans so fearful of being marked? "Why," they would say in a spirit of tolerance, "there's no such thing as an American—we're all so different from each other, which American are you talking about. Anyone could be us. Anyone could have faith and be us, in any place, and not be named as part of a religion."

Witness: the case that addressed the constitutionality of so-called religious organizations who wished to save the souls of prisoners in state-run facilities. In this case, a voluntary "Christ-centered" program, called *the Inner Freedom Initiative Plan,* run by *Prison Fellowship Ministries*, came to the State of Iowa's prisons, wanting in.

Country religious folks and state legal folks had to decide: who could enter prisons to help the prisoners under what name, faith, or religion?

The expert witness and the judge, they disagreed. She said the judge got huffy and became his *own* expert witness. The expert witness wondered: why do they call me to trial if the judge gets huffy and wants to be his *own* expert witness, o.k., so he will have his say, anyway, regardless of what I say. "I know religion," he says. "You are only a scholarly witness. The State does not want religion in the prison, the State of Iowa's prisons were wrong to let them in, since they had no freedom to choose which treatment, which religion." The judge's words were somewhat these:

that the required religious activities made the [prison rehabilitation] program [Inner Freedom Initiative Program— a voluntary, "Christcentered"(26) program run by Prison Fellowship Ministries (PFM) and operating from 1999 to 2008] "coercive," and that prisoners had "no real choice of treatment programs because of the significant incentives to join the IFI program and the virtual absence of alternative programs." (Alexander Volokh, 25 J.L. & REL.323 (2009–10).)

The judge went by what he had known all his life: the disestablishment clause the court holds dear, which told him that if it walks like a disestablishment duck or talks like a disestablishment duck, it's an established ruling in my head waiting to come down like a dead disestablishment duck.

But the expert witness said that "disestablishment," as understood in First Amendment doctrine

may be "anachronistic as a legal project," because "separation" of religion from government is best suited for "premodern, hierarchical, and institutionalized religion," not "individual religion."

While establishment doctrine is well suited for combating the inroads of institutionalized religion, it cannot combat *individualized* religion "without violating personal integrity, an integrity acknowledged in the right to privacy and… freedom of speech and of association." (Alexander Volokh, Book Review of WINNIFRED FALLERS SULLIVAN, PRISON RELIGION: FAITH-BASED REFORM AND THE CONSTITUTION (2009)), 25 J.L. & REL.323 (2009–10).)

Never mind, the Prison Fellowship Ministries' Inner Change Freedom Initiative Plan said, we'll pass or slide by under the radar here, we're just Americans, we will help the prisoners help themselves and change, for their freedom, their inner freedom, that's common, that's American.

(Common Supermen, they were, Carlos thought, in their travels, able to leap tall institutions for their faiths, Carlos thought, and then mouthed what he heard):

*Is there such a kind as the un-American*

*No*

*How can you say there's no such kind.*

*Because they won't have it.*

*Who*

*The Left and the Right. The Left and the Right are one on this one.*

*Which ones*

*The New Men: They say: Everyone's gonna be an American. They say: the State of Iowa's Prisons let the Fellowship's Ministers in*

*Where*

*In one wing of the prison*

*What else does the State of Iowa's Prisons' say*

*They say: Come into one wing of the prison, Fellows: you're no religion, you're whatever, you're here to improve our men and free them, on the inside*

*What do the New Men say*

*They say: Whatever. They say thank you: to redeem freedom is American, is American and more than American, is Christian and more than Christian-American, is, whatever*

*Do they say this freely*

*On the inside*

*Do they say "Christian" in prison*

*No*

*Why not*

*To redeem more New Men—they never say "Christian." They say: in the State of Iowa's prisons, whatever religion, everyone's gonna be an American.*

## Third Testimony

They won't have it

What

The un-American or children

Why children

Because children are too young

Too young?

Yes, too young to choose to be Born Again

What do the New Men have, then

The Inner Change Freedom Initiative Plan

For whom

The New Men to Come

What do they say

The New Men among them—say: we give you the Inner Change Freedom Initiative Plan, we do no harm, we sail on, without children…

## The New Men's Streaming Missionary Sidebar

*our workshops like freedom ships, we argue before the law, we do no harm, faith based on no religion, whatever it takes to redeem men in prison, to make it in prison as it is on earth then, to argue before the law, we say: redemption embeds no inmate conversion, only personal transformation, no acceptance of Christ, only one person's civilizing rights, no one on one knee, only personal responsibility, integrity, honesty, productivity, can-do American values we do no harm with yes we can with these New Men do even more than make them Christian or American we can make them Universal, impossible to be un-Universal, to be kicked out of an un-inclusive Universe, downright un-American in fact to be getting the boot out of the bed we all lie in the law we argue for among these New Men to be for whatever religion impossible to be against them all civilizing in common improving themselves in one wing of the prison if they can Why you ask because we say Come in, Fellows. Everyone is welcome: Left and Right are one on this one. It's like K's chaplain said: "The court wants nothing from you. It receives you when you come and it dismisses you when you go."*

## Fourth Testimony
## (the New Men's inmates speak)

*In the name of who do they come into the prisons to improve us*

*Seuss*

*Who*

*Dr. Seuss—*

*Why*

*He's a can-do honest American guy. He can change us. Improve us. As if we were children.*

*No, this can't be the name they say to the State of Iowa when they come into the prisons to change us*

*Why*

*He's child's play and we're no children, we can choose*

*Choose?*

*To be Born Again*

*So what name do they say*

*They can't*

*Why*

*Because they're bound by the split between church and state*

*So what do the New Men do*

*They say no name: they only say: Bible values stand for who we are*

*But in the name of who*

*They say: we can't tell you*

*Why*

*Because the New Men say: for now, you are welcome to your own story, you choose:*

*Can we? Can we? Yes, we can. We can change, we can improve, American values and Universal values: one and the same: just "think left and think right and think low and think high. Oh, the thinks you can think up if only you try!"*

*To say yes?*

*To say yes we can, to say it to the New Men, and then we can*

*Can do what*

*Can make it happen, thank Him, in prison as it is on earth then*

*Thank who*

*Jesus, who can be chosen*

*But not named*

*Yes, before the law this is no child's play*

*Why*

*Because in prison you must be free to not name Him if you want to change*

*Like adults?*

*Yes, like adults, living or not, now or then, today or tomorrow, it doesn't matter, but no children can be born again or can be free to choose*

*Who says*

*Evangelicals*

*Even angels?*

*Yes, even angels are adults born again, free to choose. But children cannot be free to choose*

*Where*

*In the State of Iowa, in one wing of the prison, among the New Men, they say:*

*"We argue for freedom to inner-change and not to name Him before the law"*

*Who*

*They say: we can't tell you*

*(But it's really Jesus, no?)*

*Yes*

*Where*

*Before the law, in the State of Iowa, in one wing of the prison*

*On the inside*

*Yes*

*What else do they say*

*Among the New Men?*

*Yes*

*They say: whatever religion,*

*Never name Him*

*But do come in*

(First to Fourth Testimony after Winnifred Fallers Sullivan)

## Fifth Testimony (catch-rime)

Who are the New Men

Some of them are "Eugens"

Who?

"Eugens"—short for…

What?

What it is… the Eugenics Men among us or, as they say in America, *Everyman-Under-The-Good-Endowed-Nation-State* is…

King?

Rising

Having Risen?

Like the Messiah is…

Everyman?

Everyman under the hood, in the hood, under the good-endowed-nation-state is…

The thing?

The important thing is…

The American?

Is good when good means well

Well, then, the Eugens can't be good Americans, since there are differences among them, regions and religions… They include. Me. You. Everyman. They're not pure. We can count them in, no?

For sure, except one thing

What?

The pure thing is to win

Where?

Where there's equality of condition

## Sixth Testimony

Where there's equality of condition

Count the Americans in, no

Yes, but with differences

Yes, they've much to say

It is good, no, and they include, no

Everyman

All the time—unconditional

Yet Hannah worries

Who

Hannah among the Eugens—she worries

She's different than the men among them, no

For sure

Why

She worries where there's equality of condition…

Where men *mean* well?

Where thoughts are pure

Where even races mingle?

Unconditional

Yes

Yet she worries

Why

Because they occlude

What

They breed

For sure?

They win

The thing?

The important thing is…

To breed among differences?

To improve

What it is?

To be sure

What it is

Where there is

Sameness of opinion

.

## Seventh Testimony

"The year of Harvard's Tercentenary, 1936–1937, was also the tercentenary of a great intellectual event. Three hundred years ago the rational foundations of modern science were established. It was then that the '*Weltanschaung*' which lies at the root of our modern universities were first put into a book. Its author had intended to write some comprehensive volumes under the proud title, *Le Monde*. But that philosopher, René Descartes, was dissuaded by religious dangers from publishing them in full, and limited his task to the famous *Discourse de la Methode*. In it the great idealistic postulate of the *Cogito ergo sum* was formulated, and therewith the program of man's scientific conquest of nature. Descartes' '*Cogito ergo sum*' opened the way to three hundred years of incredible scientific progress…

Both the *Credo ut intelligam* ['I have faith in order that I may come to understand'] and the *Cogito ergo sum* ['I think, therefore I am'] worked very well for a time. However, finally the *Credo ut intelligam* led to the Inquisition and the *Cogito ergo sum* to the ammunition factory. The progressive science of our days of aircraft-bombing has progressed just a bit too far into the humanities, precisely as theology had dogmatized just a bit too much when it built up its inquisition. When Joan of Arc was questioned under torture, her theological judges had ceased to believe. When Nobel Prize winners produced poison-gas, their thinking was no longer identified with existence."[4]

—Eugen Rosenstock-Huessy (Harvard Lecturer, 1933, '34) from "Farewell To Descartes"

4. Fritz Haber, winner of the Nobel Prize in Chemistry "for the synthesis of ammonia from its elements," pioneered the use of mustard/nerve gas in World War I.

"I knew a man named Eugen," he said

Among the Eugens?

Yes, but different

How

Of other stock

What stock

Rosenstock-Huessy stock

Eugen Rosenstock-Huessy stock?

Yes, you could say

What did he say?

"I am an impure thinker," he said, "Farewell to Descartes,"
he said "I think therefore I am," no more of that, he said

Where

Among the Eugens in the Harvard aether, in 1936, he said

What of it

Harvard and Descartes—1636–1936—300 years of it

Of what

"Of the aether," he said, "I am an impure thinker," he said,
in the Harvard aether

Among the Eugens?

For sure, 300 years of them

Progress

To be sure, by far—hearing they think and think and think

they can and because they do they think they are…

The shit?

For sure

Rumors among promises of poison gas in the air

Before the war

For sure, he said, "thinking no longer identified with existence," he said

What it is

They call noble

What it is

"They call noble," he said, "Farewell to Descartes," he said, "Conant and the Eugens think hard to get it," he said, "noble"

Conant?

Conant among the Noble Dead, Harvard's head, 1936

And before that

Pure groundwork before the war

Before the war?

1917

Who

Captain Conant the Chemist

Harvard's future head?

Laying the groundwork

For what

To be sure

What it is… was

Mustard gas / laying down / the nobled dead

Before he was Harvard's head?

Among the Noble Eugens

Pure

For sure

Therefore they are

What it is

The shit

*Heisse Scheisse* and Noble

"Gas," he never said

Who

"I was gassed at Verdun, 1917," he never said

Who

Eugen Rosenstock-Huessy

When did he never say it

1936

To whom

Conant among the Eugens

What did he say instead

"I am an impure thinker," he said, "Farewell to Descartes," he said

Where

At Harvard

And the year after?

He's kicked out of it

**Opening Statement:**

To those whose memory may not go back to the events of 1917, a little history might help. Today these events would be called facts on the ground, what comes to be what we live with in the wake of what we think and talk through, in the abstract. At times, these facts are anticipated, at times they are built slowly, like settlements, over time, and usually no one notices, or, more to the point, the rhetoric in the air distracts from the scene so that no one acts in time to stop them, so tension builds, until the ground swells, and the bodies are suddenly bloated, or, as one later lyric laid bare to recall it, the mustard gas / laying down / the nobled dead / at Verdun, enough for us to ask, as if of ghosts: where did all these dead neighbors in the world come from, all of a sudden, so that we return in memory and speech across the ground where no one passed (*No Pasarán!*), since a return to civil discourse is what is wanted, at this time, in history.

And to those whose memory may not go back to the events of 1933—here Hitler is not the issue—to the election of James Conant as head of the Harvard College, formerly Captain Conant the Younger, as he was called in 1916 and who, at the time, upon meeting Fritz Haber the elder in the city of Leipzig, one chemist to another, with much to think and talk through, listening to each other with interest as they spoke their gaseous inventions, with nothing but their thoughts in the air as though they did not even have to be there in time among the facts on the ground, one later lyric laid bare to recall it—the mustard gas / laying down / the nobled dead...

And to those whose memory may not go back to the events of 1946–47, who may not remember even further back how the progressive science of the first days of aircraft-bombing had progressed just a bit too far into the humanities, who have no time to care or to distinguish who the Americans and un-Americans among us were in 1946–47, are, may be, a bit puzzled, a bit young, may wonder—"Why am I here? Of what use is a liberal arts education in the twenty-first century?"—I have—what it is is—an old letter from Carlos ben [בן] Carlos Rossman, who was once given the facts straight up through his namesake, the good Dr. Carlos, "a little history, a little Shakespeare," he said,[5] "never hurt anyone," or put another way, "First, you are liberalized, then you are professionalized," which sounded like a plan, to be sure, to be pure, sounded a bit like electroshock therapy for the deeply studied, whose memory may not go back…

---

5. The good doctor was good with advice. Once he told Anglo the younger: "Son, though there is a desire on the part of the highly organized man to breed with peasant girls, remember, if you do we will abandon you to America, where much will be expected of you, and where, you should know, certain vastly important strains of men may die out due to the lack of the penetration of their highly specialized reproductive material into adequate receptors, unless we screw each other over and over until—you should be warned—the pure products of America go crazy."

# 5

# Facts on the Ground

*I think if you burn the facts long and hard in yourself as crucible you'll come to the few facts that matter. And then fact can become fable again.*

—*Carlos Karl Olson*

*America was fable before it became fact…*

—*Robert Payne*

Levitating in the blues, seeing the sky she came from color-tone the sea of our time, Hannah wrote missives home:

Dear Mothership,

It is almost impossible even now to describe what actually happened on that day, April 1, 1958. Television was as television always does: for us, for them, a form of address to undress the natives of their own skin by getting under it—in the American grain, images of tin crowned women graying under their crowns, pitiful tales told, pomp and circumstance all around them, applause meters for their woes, tears on their pillows. And for ours? We were captured as any creatures who had just arrived, the *arrivants*. And we were awed.

Smiled.

\*

Dear Mothership,

It's been over a half century since we landed in the Americas, and on the one hand nothing much has changed, or is it just the facts on the ground having swollen like ice floes without anyone noticing being carried…

And the persons swim.

And the motto is: the biggest loser still wins.

\*

Dear Mothership,

      When the biggest loser still wins, it is as if "Would you like to be Queen for a day"? were still overheard over 50 years after it debuted on television, although the Queen is no longer "the man," but an out-of-home homeowner, for whom the prize can be a home and a camera-ready face. In America, he hears, it's a fact: all will be lifted in their difference: no shame in the game to be losing where there is equality of condition among rivals—if only they save face. And smile. Where there is sameness of opinion in difference.

      In style.

\*

Dear Mothership,

That same smile, to what end
—we asked
so Alexis said: at the birth of the alien republic, to convince the American without coercing him
—to not go contrary
when social conditions are equal that same smile
Uncle Hermann said has "its ambiguity"
in the land of plenty (Carlos Karl said):
it has friends

*Whenever equality becomes a mundane fact in itself, without any gauge by which it may be measured or explained, then there is one chance in a hundred that it will be recognized simply as a working principle of a political organization in which otherwise unequal people have equal rights; there are ninety-nine chances that it will be mistaken for an innate quality of every individual, who is 'normal' if he is like everybody else and 'abnormal' if he happens to be different. This perversion of equality from a political into a social concept is all the more dangerous when a society leaves but little space for special groups and individuals, for then their differences become all the more conspicuous.*

—*Arendt*

*People laugh at us because we're different. We smile at them because they're the same.*

—*Amish*

Carlos ben [בן] Carlos Plays Badminton Upstate
While Dreaming of the American Unprecedented
Conditions of Equality Down-Under in the
So-Called Jewish State

Badminton birdies like clowns' noses flipped freely in mid-
air over the whited bungalows in Ellenville, New York, and,
when they landed, Hannah turned to Carlos and remembered what Alexis had imagined at the birth of the alien republic. Hannah asked: "What happens to us under the
unprecedented conditions of equality?" Carlos looked mute.
So she asked again, differently: "What fables do we come
to remember from the facts on the ground?"

In his muteness, dust in the air and a flowering desert
on his mind, Carlos remembered how one country could
become fabled depending on how it used the facts of another. If it desired, Israel—the so-called Greater Judea and
Samaria—could become America, or at least New York,
which was the most the average Greater Judean and Samar-
ian knew anyway—of America. "I love New York, I just
came back from there, it's just like here in Tel Aviv, but without the wars, without the fear," Guy, the teenage boy, had
said, and which was the most the average Israeli wanted—
like pizza.

"New York without the fear?" he mumbled, in disbelief.
Before 9/11, Carlos poorly remembered, it used to be only
the people upstate, where the flags flew high over the
porches, who were afraid of coming into the big city. And
he asked himself in his memory: how many New Yorkers
really saw themselves as Americans back then, and how

many proudly claimed to be un-American in order to distinguish themselves from Iowans or Texans, the way Iowans and Texans distinguished themselves from New Yorkers? The fact was: no one these days remembered this vision of New York outside America, and it was only when the fear arrived that the flags came to distinguish the Island.

Yes, well, let's do the math, Carlos thought, and see if it is possible for one land to become fabled from the facts of another, its idol.

Carlos thought: If 10 percent of New Yorkers are Jews—citizens of the American Republic—and 14 percent of Israelis are Muslims who are citizens of the Jewish State[6]—often in America called the 51st state—then what do these comparable numbers tell us, Carlos asked himself, about how, in becoming like America, Israel could be free, mathematically?

Your analogies are lazy and imperfect, he overheard, they will never work out in the real world, among the facts on the ground as we know them.

Which is why, Carlos thought, we needed to create another real world from the facts on the ground as we could know them. America, he had heard, wherever its dream migrated, was what you made of it. And he wanted to make something of it.

He remembered that, in 1958, when the family had first landed, his mother would ignore the crosses on the Brooklyn steeples, shy away from them on their walks or, more to the point, skulk in the shadows of their towering presence until later that evening she bent to light a menorah privately

6. 20 percent of present-day Israel is comprised of Palestinians, whom the state calls the Arab citizens of Israel. 70 percent of those are Muslims. If we do the math, they are 14 percent of present-day Israel.

in her home. She wanted no one to notice the lighting.

But years after they landed in the mothership, during Hanukkah, Carlos reflected on his friend Hannah's different, more twenty-first-century experience, when she witnessed the fabled menorahs in New York City pave the streets, lighting them as if with gifts of gold. They showcased the night windows of Pakistani restaurants in mid-town. They were tucked away in corner spaces among boxes of fried plantains in Chinese-Cuban delis. They graced the ticket grilles at Grand Central Station. They appeared over the metal detectors inside the Queens County courthouse and across the street in the blue-tinted windows of the Colombian bails bondsmen. They knew enough not to compete with Christmas trees so much as condition individuals to the demands of a society, so Hannah once said, to make a home for 10 percent of a people as if they were just a given no one needed to remind anyone of. Even if their initial appearances in the non-Jewish world were just good for business or marketing relations, even if that's why they replicated and started to shine on the streets of the metropolis, so be it, in a future time the city would look bare in winter without them—this electric, one would not even need to say religious, light, present in the mass luminosity of spirit the objects reflected, objects no one even noticed were present. And that was the point: in the twenty-first century, no one even noticed they were present—only the mass luminosity of the spirits they reflected.

Carlos thought: it is my lonely American dream—to reinvent the Jewish State from the American facts on the ground. "New York without the fear?" cried the teenager from Tel Aviv.

The birdies landed. The flags flew only upstate. He thought about his friend Ismail from Palestine, who once said he did not want to die as just another number on the streets of New York.

"Yes, exactly," Ismail said, "I think I know where you're going."

"Do you?" Carlos asked.

"You want to know the Islamic object equivalent to the menorah."

In as many as years as it took the occluded menorah to come across the blocks and light the streets of New York, we could, Carlos suggested to Ismail, offer the Ramadan *fanoos*, the oil-lit lantern, to any city in the so-called Jewish State, to all the shops, hang them in the kitchens of the Chinese restaurants whose chefs knew enough about doing good business to accommodate the tastes of the natives by over-salting the won ton and the egg rolls, display them in the windows of the homes of the Thai guest workers, in the Jewish nursing homes commanded by Russian arrivals ministered and absorbed as de facto citizens and pseudo-Jews before they started overcrowding the once empty monasteries in the North, in the bakeries blessed by the rabbis, in Swiss boutiques on the Merkaz, we could come to light the Ramadan *fanoos*, the oil-lit lantern here in its multiple appearances, Carlos thought, as in New York they lighted the Menorah wherever it could be found in *its* multiple appearances, we could be free in the so-called Jewish State like the people were in America, in New York, "to be New York without the fear"—like a gift, as if the fear of the State were no longer present.

# Ismail Smiles like an American at Israeli Passport Control While His Children Absorb the Language of It All

## 1

Ismail hikes through the garden sculptures of Jaffa to reach his home: a towering communist-style block of apartments overlooking the sea on a street signed Ben Gurion-Balfour Boulevard, coupling the name of the first prime minister with the 1917 Balfour Declaration which gave the so-called Jewish State its *raison d'etre*.

Ismail's fable can be written out of his family's resemblance to the multicultural facts of America in Israel—and Israelis *love* America—where he is denied a Palestinian country in his own land. If you want the facts as they can be found on the ground in America, go to his Jaffa, Carlos says, his Palestine. The American Dream is alive and flowering there.

Ismail has never thought to hike towards the American Embassy downtown, lay down his backpack, take out a map, and make the case for his version of the American Dream Homeland abroad here in Jaffa, which really would not need a map, just an ear to hear it. If he were Carlos, here are the facts of the case he would present to the Embassy downtown, as one carries a menorah like a gift into the Queens County Courthouse in New York:

"A Muslim man born in Jaffa," Carlos tells the sleepy American case officer in the Embassy, "Ismail marries an American Jewish woman whom he meets in Oklahoma, and through her becomes an American citizen, while she converts to Islam and with him returns to the Israeli Jewish State. Eventually they have children, who, in time, are taught perfect Arabic, English, and, yes, even a little Hebrew to get by in the official language of the State. Ironically, whenever he returns home from a visit to the State of Oklahoma with his American and Israeli passports in hand and his children by his side, this Palestinian citizen of Israel must cross the grim and dour security girls at passport control, who are suspicious of him, of where he comes from, which is not the State where they come from, even though it looks like the same place."

Carlos asks him, "How do you face their suspicion each time you return?"

And Ismail says: "As an American citizen, and with my English."

"With your English?"

"Yes, I intimidate them with my English."

## 2

Once he crosses the border, Hebrew is heard everywhere. But for Ismail's children, in the fantasies Carlos constructs, this is a Hebrew comparable to the English one hears outside any barrio in America.

One day Berri, who was born in Israel but no longer lives there, takes a taxi from his mother's nursing home and visits Carlos and Ismail at the apartment on Ben Gurion-Balfour Boulevard, which historicizes the sameness of one people in one land through a street sign, and which means any sign of Ismail's presence becomes all the more conspicuous on this street he crosses to return to his home.

The taxi drops Berri off in front of the apartment building, and he walks up the stairs before reaching an open door on the third floor. Giggling children around him, Berri is asked to slip off his sandals at the doormat and greets Carlos and Ismail, who are eating almonds at the threshold:

"Come in," Ismail says, "please. This is my daughter, Rayan. She is eight."

Turning to Rayan, Ismail says in perfect American English:

"Rayan, this is Berri. He is visiting from America but he was actually born here in Israel."

Rayan stands on her toes and Ismail bends his head to hear her whispering in his ears.

He laughs.

"Why is she giggling?" Berri asks.

"She wants to know why, if Berri was born in Israel, he does not speak Arabic?"

## Carlos Smiles like Uncle Hermann
## at Passport Control

In Greater Judea and Samaria, across the speech-grille, Carlos shows his American passport and is asked by the grim and dour security girl:

"Vat iz zee purpuss ov your visit?"
"I am a pilgirim
Come to bring
The Arab Spring"

Carlos ben [בּן] Carlos Trades Places with a Potential
Immigrant Going the Other Way (like Himself)
and Considers His Right of Return in Exchange for a
Landlord Leaving towards America

"Expect it: the customer here is always wrong," the grim
and dour security girls told Carlos at passport control.

The train from the airport took him to a seacoast city
in Greater Judea and Samaria, where he walked a mile in
the heat to see about renting a room which had been ad-
vertised in the local paper. Coming to a gate on a block
where evergreen branches hung crossing each other into the
center of the street, he rang the buzzer, with one American
and one so-called native flag above him, entangled in the
wind. An elderly woman did not so much biblically answer
the call, that is, open the gate, as stand at the top of some
stairs, with a scowl on her face and two small children in
party dresses on either side of her with even cuter scowls on
their faces, as an Arab workman in overalls stood behind
her, a heavy work belt dragging his pants down, while jackhammers behind the house unnerved the whole gathering,
all called to account for Carlos's presence.

"Yes, what do you want?" she shouted.

"I'm here to see the room," he shouted back, thinking
to do business, to give you good business, lady. (He wondered if she knew the American cliché: "the business of
America is business.")

"Did you make an appointment?"

"Well, no, but…"

"You know," she said, "I'm watching these children, I'm

feeding the worker lunch, the house is being remodeled and I'm trying to pack for a big trip. I'm busy, can you come back later…" as she yelled over the jackhammers and refused to move from the top of the stairs.

"I've just arrived in the country and I wanted to take a quick look at the room—for future reference," he barked back.

"Well," she laughed, "I need to pay the rent for present reference."

"Well, I have a place to stay at the moment, but I'm just shopping around," as they say ("as they say in America" is what he really thought).

"Well, this is not the most convenient time. I will be leaving for America in a few days, I'm in a bit of a rush, I can't accommodate every request to see the room, but I guess you can take a peek, though hurry it up."

"Every request to see the room?" Carlos thought, puzzled. Are there really that many requests, since he saw no one else at the gate and she carried no phone. He thought: when she arrives in America, how will she accommodate herself to the customer who is always right, the native (like himself) who won't be refused service?

She walked to the gate, opened it, and he hurried to the back of the house, where he saw a spacious room with, of all things, a stair-master and a wide flat-screen television, strange for a bedsit. As the noise got louder and he checked out the rest of the room, she followed him, as if waiting for a deposit, and he cupped his hands over his ears to hear himself mouth a few muted, distressed words to her over the jackhammers. She shot a humiliating gaze at him, and shouted:

"What, you haven't even rented the room and already you're complaining?"

## Carlos Returns to America to Dream the Right to Privacy and Eat Out among the Guest Workers

The silent guest worker waitress at Panini's is always hovering—stuffing napkins in the condiment holder at Carlos's table, begging to take his plate away, visibly disappointed when he says "no, I'm keeping it," then moving to another customer and unrolling his table umbrella when the fog rolls in to this gated American beach community.

The irony is she has not, as the immigration minutemen of the twenty-first century like to think, crossed the border for a free meal ticket or to take "our" right to work away. Just the opposite—she works like a real American, perpetually trying to work in the country's image of itself, a cog in the wheel, just doing her job under the unprecedented conditions of equality. She is the story of the overworker in America. She gets Carlos's muffins to him as soon as he asks, and he wonders how, in a few years, she will articulate her frustrations at being treated like a slave, like any other guest worker in America. Will she be free enough to use the idioms she has studied in her community college ESL class, if she gets humiliated enough by the job?

Carlos imagines that one day he will hear her say something to the cook like "Boy, that customer outside is sooner or later going to get his *comeuppance*, if he's not careful"—and she'll be facile enough with the language to deny she said this when confronted by her boss, "Did you say that," he'll interrogate her, and she'll say: "No, I'd never say that, boss, really, I said, that customer outside is sooner or later going to get his *muffins*." And all is well, for the moment, for this future moment...

... But for now, all this time on the outside she has been eyeing her boss through the window, reflecting her need to look to him as if she's busy and, in the process, disturbing the customers. It's too much. Carlos thinks: she might get the picture if someone went up to her boss, maybe someone like Carlos who is just trying to eat his meal in peace, and told the boss that her determination to have him see her work (like a real American) is really getting on people's nerves. Someone should do something about her. She can't be here enough, Carlos grimaces, and it's this way with most industrious service workers in America, he mumbles to himself—this denial of our right to privacy.

## Carlos Marvels at a Nation of Doers

When he was younger, Carlos saw Americans take to the road, fly to Europe, eat at diners or luncheonettes, even the working class. Over the years, because these people were moving in all directions, he expected the vocabulary like the people to move, to change and expand as it moved, but it only diminished.

Where one used to visit Venice and marvel at the canals, now one would do Venice and move on. Where one used to eat out once upon a time, now one would do lunch all the time. This was far different, Carlos thought, from the way things were done in his time, when the only legitimate thing one could really do was drugs.

These days, however, it seemed the people around him had become a nation of doers, but could express it less and less or, in expressing it, would go over the top, turned into what Carlos called American exclamatory friendly: evident when grownups like their teenage children could not help but seeing this that or the other as "sooo cute" or "soooo amazing." Or when a young woman dropped a cell phone right underneath her seat on the train and a bystander picked it up and the woman, not missing a beat, said: "Thank you sooo much." Or when a waitress who in any other country would just be doing her job brought a diner a napkin and heard in return "Thank you sooooo much."

"Thank you soooo much," Carlos heard the young blond girl say when the waitress handed her the menu at the local café.

Depressed yet hopeful, she looked at the menu while talking to the waitress: "I'm allergic to egg yolk, so, do you do egg whites here?"

Again, Carlos thought, this was far different from the way things were done in his time, when the only hopeful thing one could do when depressed was sing along with the Supremes, asking: "why you do me like you do, when I've been true."

As many people as were doing it or seeming to do it like the nouveau-doers, there were other people in the early twenty-first century who were doing nothing, adopting aristocratic stances yet doing things vicariously, as if they were reflections of Bertolt Brecht's Mr. Keuner, who said: "I, too, once adopted an aristocratic stance (you know: erect, upright, and proud, head thrown back). I was standing in rising water at the time. I adopted this stance when it rose to my chin." These vicarious stances were evident, it seemed to Carlos, in how they named their children and called them and did things with them without really going anywhere, knighting them with awesome names Carlos had never heard before, like Austin and Conner and Alexis and Brady, who came to this working class of America from what seemed to be a television soap opera cast.

So Carlos marveled at the cast.

Of another class.

Of the desire to do things like another class.

## Carlos Eats among the Simple Patrons When the Dwellers Come Down the Hill like Parrots

In America, Carlos wonders, and asks because his friends work there: are well-marketed cafés just family cooks who hire two Mexicans and then prepare food as poor folk do when they play to the rich they are subject to?

The old and nouveau well-to-do…

dwell on the hill near the old telegraph poles where the parrots alight, and the nouveau well-to-do die not knowing—the exploits of the poor case in point:

there is an Italian café down the hill, home cooking from the motherland that "embodies," the food critic writes, "the soul of Tuscany," his column on the café wall of fame. The food critic has brought it upon us—the simple patrons—

to be mobbed with dwellers. Human parrots on the ground, the dwellers come alive in their Tuscany on the West Coast of America and Carlos like an angel has landed there to observe them gather like a class.

## Carlos Learns How the Classes Separate European from Chinese Laundry

In the Chinese hood this once Italian retreat in America has become, sleeveless white t-shirts and linen hang from the fire escape across the alley from the Italian café, and Carlos observes the bejeweled American woman who is about to cross the threshold into the café but first looks up at the laundry in wonder and smiles and says: "How European!"

## Carlos Considers the Possibilities of Spotting an Un-American at Santorini's Italian No ~~Free~~ Wi-Fi Café

At Santorini's, the wall sockets have been plugged, and the young wireless Americans of all classes cannot comprehend it. "Doesn't this owner want to do business," they think, their computer bags slung over their shoulders as they walk past the window with the new sign, the "free" now crossed out and the "No" just added: "No ~~Free~~ Wi Fi."

Carlos walks in and introduces himself to Santorini, who says: "This is where all the Italian tourists come to get the real thing. I don't care if the Americans like me, they should like my espressos and cannolis. Anyway, they're killing themselves with sweeteners and always asking how I am and then they just sit around all day with their laptops and put too much milk and sugar in their Americanos. Yeah, can you believe it, this is an Italian café and they're asking for Americanos."

A bearded guy bearing the ventilated cardboard box he lives in stumbles through the door and looks at the No ~~Free~~ Wi-Fi sign on the window, his speech sounding slowly drunk or stroked but nevertheless astonished: "No free waffles anymore?" he asks. "Don't you got no more free waffles," and a bit more desperately, "you used to have free waffles, man, what happened?" and Santorini reaches for his iron. "Please—have a seat."

"This guy's fuckin' incredible," the Americans mumble, as they walk off into the street. "Doesn't he want our business? It's as if he's sticking his finger in our faces."

"Wi Fi?" he exclaims, giving them the sign—and turns his back to the traffic.

Santorini Answers the Dwellers and their Tourist
Brochures with the Hanging Threat of Chinese
Dwarf Bananas

"How can it be that, in America, of all places, they're taking
the food out of my customers' mouths," Santorini screams,
"the Dwellers on the hill there, they'll see soon enough what
happens to the old neighborhood when the real *turista*
come."

The Dwellers list Santorini's in every tourist book of the
city. It has occupied this Italian ground since 1860, the old-
est café in San Francisco, original home to the Italian newspaper's printing press. But if he doesn't pay someone off
soon, anyone, there'll be no permit for food or wine or live
music, no permission to cook, no up-to-code chimney for
the steak smoke to disappear through.

The fact is: Santorini also wants to disappear like smoke
through a chimney or to steaming Manila if he has to,
where his wife and children live in an American mansion
and, if he becomes a citizen through his Filipino-American
wife, he can join them there, without returning every six
months to renew his green card. He can join them as a citizen outside America and leave for the Dwellers a gesture
of contempt, a future where Chinese dwarf bananas are
hanging from the awning of his Italian storefront, inside of
which is tacked on the wall the 1931 photo of a crowd
listening to Mussolini outside the café, which is blaring his
radio speech into the street, the same photo which also
graces the brochures at the Chamber of Commerce, where
the Dwellers visit to discuss the capital of the city.

"They'll see," he says, "what happens to their city when the tourists look into their tour guides for Santorini's and then look up and all they see are bananas, Chinese dwarf bananas. I don't need no permit," he says, "they'll see soon enough and I'll be vacationing in the shade of a mansion in steaming Manila."

To make his point, every Sunday, as the trombones and trumpets of the Green Street Mortuary band lead a Chinese procession of limousine mourners as if through Kafka's Nature Theatre of Oklahoma, Santorini steps into the street, points like a conductor to the trombones guiding the mourners and, shouting, waves the throng of Midwestern *turista* inside:

"Listen, everyone. Everyone is welcome. Look" (and with his arms in a downbeat to the band of mourners in the street): "*Live* music at Santorini's!"

## Carlos Brushes Up Against the Un-American Pintore Anti-Fascista and Wonders Why More Americans Are Not Screaming "You Fascist" Anymore

At Santorini's, Carlos sits upstairs by the window, watching the numbers on the roofs of the buses passing by, numbers painted there so that the buses can be tracked by air in case the transit system is hijacked.

Downstairs, the black-robed Greek artist paints portraits on the café wall and stares outside and starts pointing and waving his brushes in protest at the scene outside.

"Look at those cops out there. Eight cops, four on each side of the street, checking the buses going in both directions. Cops getting on as passengers get off, checking bus transfers, with nothing better to do. There are cocaine dealers all over this city, and they're checking fake bus transfers? You got to be kidding. This is not why mother escaped the Greek fascists, to come over here to America to see the fascist pigs getting off on innocent riders."

It's true. Carlos looks below. The Chinese and the homeless are all gesticulating, but the cops' gesticulations look more threatening—questioning individuals within the throng of passengers—maybe because their hands will come to rest on the holsters at their hips. The street scene is "alive" with these facts.

*No doubt*, he marks in his notebook, *everyone's justifying their transfers*. The buses could go rogue.

*

In the 1964 LeRoi Jones play called "Dutchman," the hip white seductress Lula says "You fascist" to the younger, buttoned-up black man Clay, and Carlos wonders what she means, calling him a fascist, "cold as ashes." Maybe she believes he needs to play up his desire for order and rigor to show he can act Middle-Class White and Responsible, to show he could rationalize her murder in some future time as she does his in this present time. Or maybe she is just throwing out epithets.

For Carlos, the word is only a reminder: hip people used to call police fascists.

*

The Spartan painter, tall, with long, curly dark hair, wears a sword hanging from his belt, and inside long cylindrical bags carries his brushes over his shoulders like Torah scrolls. For months he has been painting portraits on the café wall of Santorini's. Santorini has requested a scene of two Native Americans on the wall, a chief and his wife, and the Spartan obliges. He is being paid, daily, in full. It is only in the last few days, since Carlos arrived and heard the story, that the Spartan has been screaming and madly waving his brushes at the cops outside.

"Hey, you, *anti-fascista spartano pintore* ("anti-fascist spartan painter"), Santorini calls out to the Spartan, "calm down, man, relax, please, you're disturbing the customers, they have a right to privacy. To each his own, man…" Santorini says, "thank you."

But the Spartan can't stop himself and doesn't understand when "thank you" means "no thank you."

Carlos walks in one afternoon and Santorini laughs and tells him he fired the Spartan for "disturbing the peace" just before the painting was finished. There's the chief, yes, his wife, the peace pipe in his hand. But the wife is not complete: maybe her eyes are missing.

As if guided by a law which demands he shoo customers out of a café in which a shrouded corpse rests, and as if saying in perfect American cop-talk to his customers, "O.k., folks, move on, there's nothing to see here," Santorini completes the picture by making his words come true, "Nothing to see here, folks," erasing the wife, lacquering her with black paint while whistling the Rolling Stones' "Paint it Black." In the chief's hand, he draws a pink Italian newspaper rag resembling *La Gazzetta della Sport*, born in the late nineteenth century and these days published in eight cities on pink newsprint. As the chief reads the inside scoop on nineteenth-century local reaction to the Patwin-speaking Isidora Filomena de Solano's words "I do not like the white man because he is a liar and a thief," not to mention, Carlos guesses, a fascist, Santorini makes sure his customers are reading his words on the outside of the sheet, right under the peace pipe, "ITALIA CAMPIONE 2010" (Italy Champion 2010).

In June 2010, before the World Cup begins, a Native American chief—a prophet from the nineteenth century—reads with a smile among the police and the anti-fascists.

Yet Carlos is curious: "Why," Carlos asks Santorini, "after the 150 years the café's been here, did you decide on this Indian chief on the wall of an Italian café? He seems a bit out of place, no?"

"Hey," Santorini smiles and gestures to the wall like a proud subject to his king, "our first customer in America."

## Carlos Wonders Why the Americans from Ascea Are Not Saying They Are from America

At Santorini's, Carlos waits upstairs.

A middle-aged bald, big-bellied man wearing a black and orange baseball shirt comes in with his bejeweled American wife and smiles and in a big voice asks Santorini in perfect Jersey City American: "Tell me, how do you pronounce Martino?"

"*Marteeno,*" the Salernan Santorini behind the bar comes right back at him, stressing the Italian, stretching it.

"Where you from?" the little fat guy asks.

"Ascea, near Salerno."

"Oh," he gets ready to slap him on the back, "we're cousins, I'm from Sarno! I'm Italian, like you." And he leaves, smiling, after some more small talk.

Puzzled, Carlos walks down the steps and turns at the counter to Santorini: "Where did he say he was from?"

"Sarno."

"Where is that?"

"Near Ascea, near Salerno."

"And what did he say he was?"

"Italian."

"But he couldn't even pronounce *Marteeno,*" Carlos says, stressing the Italian, stretching it the way the American claiming to be from Sarno can't.

"Hey, I don't know," Santorini says, "what can I say. It's nice. He means that's his heritage, he means he loves to be from Italy, he's proud, even though he's never been there. Italy has the best clothes, the best food, the best women, he knows it. He's proud, like me. He wants to feel special, different, but like one of us."

"But his clothes, his woman, are from *here*… from one of *us*, Americans."

"Yeah, I know. Sarno, Salerno, Marteeno, they're good to know, I suppose. They sound nice to be from if you're not from there. They do."

"Santorini, listen: say your grandmother was from America, and you lived in Ascea, could you tell an American bar owner over there that he was your cousin from here in America?

"I could but I wouldn't."

"Why not?"

"Because I'm not."

"But it's your heritage. Where's your pride in America? Your clothes? Your women? Where are they from?"

"Ascea."

## Carlos and Hannah Over-Think the Ethnic Divide

Carlos telepaths Hannah from the mothership: "To impress Santorini, I think that these American tourists are making themselves sound different, describing themselves as they would fashionable breeds of dog: *You know*, one of them adoringly faces him when she says this, *I have a bit of Scotch and Indian and French in me* as her friend chimes in, *yeah I've got some Italian in me too,* as if the two of them have been around the global block, their bodies transported to the Scotch and Indian and French pastorals of the world, although I think, my guess is, they have never foregone the exclamatory spirit of the suburbs of LA, where they are from."

"This is the trouble," Hannah thinks, "with the American's focus on the pride of the ethnic divide, the hyphenated American: it makes some of the least visible and longest mainstays of the American diverse—Scottish-American, German-American, Swedish-American, etc.—claim themselves as the world come to America yet again, as if they were forgotten reflections of today's *arrivants*."

The Newfound American digs into his own won-over self and finds that the inviting nature of the nation offers him the right to imbibe this sovereign worldly feeling of the multitudes like a mixed drink, with a little bit of this and a little bit of that in him. So Hannah thinks: "Of course, after everyone's been drinking, it all feels right, everyone seems different and welcome, and equality, like a family's choice of suburbs, becomes a mundane fact in itself."

## Carlos Meets a Londoner, a Madridian, and a Stuttgarter in an American Café

Simon, the Londoner from Toronto, says the American soccer team his team played boasted, but ultimately lost to the Canadians in "a friendly." "We showed them," he says, "but we could never have talked trash beforehand about it." "We are still upset," he says, "that we did not boast like the Americans."

Carlos asks them: "What do you notice about Americans?"

"Their confidence."

"And is that a good thing?"

"Yes, of course," the Madridian says, "In Europe, in business, we bring up a new idea and our colleagues who know everything are primed to say no. In America, everyone says yes to us, let's go for it, even if they know nothing about it."

"And you like that?" Carlos asks.

"Oh, yes," says the Stuttgarter, "we love that they boast they can get it done."

"Even if they can't? Even if they lose in 'a friendly?'"

## Carlos Hears the Hard-of-Hearing American

The height of deaf pragmatism is a language lesson in public. Every Saturday in the café, one balding man nervously working a blade like a drumstick through his fingers is teaching another older man, an American who likes to walk on tip toes, Italian or Spanish—Carlos really can't hear which through the background jazz…

They are communicating effortlessly, even though the American is making no effort: maybe he is not aware or does not care or thinks it's redundant that when learning a foreign language he should make an effort to sound somewhat like a native in that language. He pronounces the *ah* in *grazie* as if it and he were hard of hearing, *eh*? What Carlos hears, well, it's crazy, since it does not sound like Italian or Spanish but like the place in the American language where Dr. Carlos Williams said the secret lies, "in the monotony of our intonation, of much that we might tell."

Curiously, the two men understand each other no matter where the American marks the accents, as if they were agreed that to hear the music in a language was only an afterthought, *the note just after*, spoken elsewhere.

## Carlos Wonders if the American Green Card Is Good for the People from Lucca

Ten minutes after Elia's father landed at night in Lucca, he threw the car keys in the air and wanted to return to Amerika. "I am sadly disappointed in my Italian home-land," he said, "once again."

The Luccan airport rental car lady had given him the keys and so he asked, naturally, where's the car, as she pointed in the dark to ten parking lots in back of her, each the size of a soccer pitch, and said to Elia's father: "Some-where out there. Just keep clicking the door alarm on the keys and you'll find it. Ciao."

\*

Back in Amerika, Elia had told Carlos that when his father had returned to Lucca with him to renew Elia's visa, which would only last six months, the sleepy case officer at the Ital-ian consulate gave him a choice: "to stay in America, you must either find a girl to marry or get a student visa."

For the first "must," he had to pay a girl the money he earned under the table (*in nero*) at his parents' café. For the second, he had to stop working under the table at his par-ents' café in order to study full-time, which would do his parents no good, since they would have to hire someone to work in his place at the café, their expenses mounting, thus giving them even less proof that they were boosting the American economy through their foreign investment in a business, which is what the Italian consul expected of them if they were to stay, nothing less, than to show how they could boost business to make it in Amerika. Of course, these were the rules, he told Carlos.

Marry or study. Under the table (*in nero*).

"So where do you like it more: America or Italy?" Carlos asked Elia.

"If you are able to live in America, you play by the rules, everything is on the, how do you say, up and up, so you know where you stand," Elia said in model English, and Carlos wondered: "on the up and up," "to know where you stand"—is this where the American "upstanding citizen" comes from?

"Is it good to play by the rules?" Carlos asked.

"Well, yes, I mean—I know I need to marry or study to be in America. One or the other—or both," he joked, "if I want to stay. In Italy," he says, "it's different: everything changes by the minute. You never know where you stand. One minute I pay for a pizza, the next minute I ask for a fork and then it's a Euro for the fork to eat the pizza and then I drop the fork and then another Euro gone before the pizza's even touched... They call it *coperto*—a cover charge for, how do you call them in English, *the cutlery*?

"But if the baby in the high chair next to me drops the fork, well, the parents will not pay extra, no worries, we'll take care of it, the hostess says. And I see they don't pay for *the cutlery*, and that the price of the cutlery can be negotiated, except for me: one moment I have a spoon and knife in my hand, the next moment I'm alone without the cutlery and wailing like a baby in front of my thick cannellini soup."

What Elia means, Carlos thinks, is this: The consumer bureaucracy in Italy can reduce you to bawling like a baby.

"Are you saying in Italy you can't always get what you want?" Carlos asks.

"Yeah, but if you try sometimes, you get what you need."

Well, Carlos thought, that certainly did sound like the same old song, and he had heard it before. But he wanted to find out more. So one day he called and asked Hannah, who had just landed in the mothership in the dry State of Oklahoma:

"America is special, no?"

"Yes, exceptional, Carlos," as she dusted herself off after seeing a local church's "rain service," "why do you ask?"

"But the people are pragmatic?"

"Yes, they play by the rules."

"No exceptions."

"Yes, no exceptions."

"An exceptional country which makes no exceptions. How can that be?" Carlos asks.

"Because everyone is welcome."

"Without exception!"

"Fair is Square."

"Where?"

"In America."

"It is where you want the green card if you can get it," Carlos says.

"And where Santorini wants a wine permit," Elia says, "if he can get it."

"Which is what you have, right?" Carlos asks.

"Yes, we have a wine permit. The lawyers came and went. We had a hearing."

"And the judge heard you," Carlos says, "and now you have a wine permit."

"We played by the rules," Elia says, "business is good. We now serve wine with food."

"And Santorini got married," Carlos says, "and can stay, which is also good."

"Yes, he played by the rules, he married, but he has no wine permit or live music and no one has come into his café for days."

"Yes, it's sad and strange, he can stay but can't serve and you can serve but can't stay—in Amerika."

"Yes, it's sad to say goodbye, to leave America, to come in, to go out, like customers."

"Even as you serve them."

"That's my right," Elia says, "to serve wine."

"Which Santorini does not have. It's sad and strange: he has no rights but the right to stay."

"Without even the permit to cook or sing with a band in his café."

So he stays and, with his arms in a downbeat pointing at the Green Street Mortuary Band marching down the street, steps outside his café, waves his inside patrons out, and screams: "Everyone, please come in, go out. Everyone is welcome. Listen" (cueing the Mortuary Band): "*Live* music at Santorini's!"

# 6

## Fables in the Air

# Contents

## Mr. Obama's Fable for Iran's America

President Barack Hussein Obama should have listened to Abbas, Carlos's gas station mechanic:

"How curious you Americans are," Abbas said. "Iran has an election and it is contested and then hundreds of thousands of the veiled and unveiled throngs in Tehran come out in protest in the streets and America says, why won't their Supreme Leaders listen to these people who want freedom like we have it here in America," and Abbas like a human jinn wheel turns on a dime and says, "this is hard to hear this 'like we have it here in America' because only a few years earlier in a contested election in Florida your own Supreme Leaders make a decision for Mr. Bush and then no one shows up in the streets of Florida, why not, and it is enough for little Mr. Gore the loser to face the camera, conceding, for everyone to just, well, they go away, they go home."

"This should not have been my story," Abbas says to Carlos, "this should have been Mr. Obama speaking from his bully pulpit the rumor of a fable from the facts on the ground in Tehran, *his* Iranian vision of what is possible in protest for Mr. Gore and the people of America when they don't just quit and go home, and for their Supreme Leaders. This should have been," Abbas says, "his squeaky wheel getting us all the grease."

Just off the Mothership, Hannah Records the Fable of Herself and an Old Man from Another Land with a Young Skateboarder from "This Land Is Your Land"

"In my day," Hannah remembered, "on a hot summer day I saw a man named Eda in shirt sleeves with his forearm numbered and I never wondered as a child: could a whole people's forearms be numbered like this?"

"In my day," Carlos's friend Mordico said, "'Eda' meant something different: the arch-cadenced essence of Turkish poetry interiorized, like an inscription, for the soul of a people."

"In my day," the old man from another land said, "if your head was shaved and tattoos fleshed out your arm, you were either home from the Navy or the Holocaust."

"I guess," the microphone caught the old man admonishing the tattooed head-shaven skateboarder on the beach, "you don't consider the effect you have on other people's memories, do you, before you make a fashion statement?"

"The coiled blue snakes on my arm are a sign, not a fashion statement," the kid said.

"There are lots of those in the world today," the old man said, "and in America more than enough."

"Blue snakes?"

"No, signs."

"What's wrong with that?"

"Nothing—except after a while, no one notices. There are so many. Everyone makes their private my public. Every one has the same philosophy of difference in America. It's what makes them the same as they go their own way."

"You mean," the kid said, "like 'You Don't Stop Skiing Because You Get Old: You Get Old Because You Stop Skiing.'"

"Or: 'Don't Be Last.'"

"Be Upbeat."

"Don't Get Beaten."

"Don't Be a Sucker."

"Grind It Out," which it reads on the back of the young fat guy's t-shirt, as he lies on the beach.

"Just Do It."

"Well," the kid said, "I do, but I'm not into those kinds of signs. The people who wear them work *way* too hard for me, even when they're having fun. I wish they would just, like Father Guido Sarducci, *play ball*—no logos. Do you know Angelo?"

"Who?"

And the kid takes out a photo of his friend Angelo's forearm: a frozen tattooed trail of loving black spiraled inkwell memorials to his drived-by-taken-to-Oakland's-Highland-Hospital-and-pronounced-dead-on-arrival cousins.

*

"Next time you're on the scorched beach," the microphone caught the old man saying to the skateboarder, "and the sand is crawling with tattooed flesh, and the Island Emergency Ambulance Service Transport Van sirens itself by you on the boardwalk, read the words some hospital ad man spread across the back of that van: 'A Passion for Caring,' and then tell me who reads these signs as if they make a difference."

"Hey, to each his own," the kid said, flipping his board in the air.

## The Fable of the Un-American Bread Line Sovereigns

*"I take SPACE to be the central fact to man born in America, from Folsom cave to now. I spell it large because it comes large here. Large, and without mercy... Some men ride on such space, others have to fasten themselves like a tent stake to survive."*

*—Olson*

The newly arrived aged Chinese in the old American city, stare-

At everything: Children, trash cans, longhairs, skinheads.

They Tai Chi their legs in the damp air—they look down the block at you there

But they don't mean anything by it. Or they don't mean what you think.

Then what do they mean?

They do the same that the New Russian Jews do in Israel in Red Haifa Square.

Is that where they take up?

Yes.

What?

Air. Space.

Space Congregations?

Yes.

How? Who? What do they do?

Small compressed women with their wrists clasped behind their backs. They hug the earth when they walk uphill—no one gets by them from behind when they walk. They've got their own backs.

Who?

The Chinese do this in Lincoln Park Square the Jews in Red Haifa Square

And where do they go, there?

In Haifa?

Yes.

Into the market: 95 years old, the old Jew is 5'2" with her head in the air going for the crowded butcher counter in the back of the store between two giant camouflaged young soldiers who look like personal bodyguards but they're there for their own rations not for hers and she's between them she parts them they fall to the side without her even touching them they collapse like the rest of the crowd they have been hungry on line for a half hour trying to get in an order and suddenly they've fallen and she's just there, staring at the beef window, that's her space where, with her voice cutting in—"I want *that* piece of beef," she points at the glass to claim it

Rare.

What will you say of her? What will you say of them?

I will say:

And where they have taken up

Space is not there.

## Evacuation Has Its Right of Return

Carlos and Hannah remember: Over 60 years, from the 1950s to 2011, Ellenville, New York, changed, from immigrant secular Jews bungalowing it in the poor man's Catskills to bearded droves headed in Eurovans towards prime Hasidic real estate.

Carlos and Hannah don't even ask:

Anywhere in Amerika, who questions the rights of first-time buyers to claim what is theirs for the right price? And, in Israel, which loves to resemble Amerika, why should it be any different?

As Carlos watches the tattooed kids moving into a brownstone in Brooklyn's Fort Greene neighborhood, Walid emails him that the young Orthodox Jewish couple from Tel Aviv have their investors bidding on his house in the poorest Arab part of Haifa, Wadi Nisnas.

Waiting on an offer, the Israeli couple will not distinguish the right of first-time home buyers like themselves from the right of a people returning to claim "what is mine," like their grandparents.

In a time of relative peace, Tel Aviv real estate investors buy up Arab fixer-uppers for the Orthodox.

Touch a spinning blue globe and feel under trembling thumbs how evacuation has its hipster and conservative worldly simulations.

## Carlos ben [בן] Carlos Rossman Invents Baseball's the Unnatural Playing Both Ends of the Stick

*Se tutto va bene, sono rovinato*
"If everything goes o.k, I'm fucked."

As a child, leaving the mothership, Carlos ben [בן] Carlos Rossman wondered at the storm of pitching gods behind Sandy Koufax and Luis Arroyo but never needed to feel good about a Jew and a Puerto Rican to feel good enough about himself to think he might one day punch his ticket to the big show. He'd have needed their arms for that.

For sure, he did not need his own green baseball bat, given Carlos by his alien father, who had loved Amerika and its colors but was strangely deaf to the difference between wetback and greenback. Years later, Carlos could finally shape the unasked question about Amerika for his dead father: "Aba [אבא], why, unlike the young Mickey Mantle pacing for some good wood in the hollow dugouts of Spavinaw, Oklahoma, was I given my own green baseball bat upon our arrival?" Carlos wondered: did the gift stand for a color-coded alien end-of-time baseball fable his father wanted Carlos to recover for the Americas in good time, or was it meant to stop him in his own time from being chosen to play? Because if that was the point, then it worked.

As sheepish as he was showing up with his bat and surplus cap among the unpainted, sawdusty pines the other boys carried, Carlos played to his backward, backyard strengths: a left-hander with an arm strong enough to play third, which no left-hander ever played because of "the turn."

"You can't play third," the guys shouted "because you're a leftie, man, you gotta make 'the turn,' you're gonna have to force the throw and, look around, Carlos, do you see any natural left-handed third basemen," their arms canvassing the air in one sweeping motion.

In practice, his left arm never forced it. Years later, he thought: why do people assume that if it looks unnatural it's forced? The turns and throws were smooth and wicked, making up the time it took to make the full circle turn it took to shut the other guys up.

But they didn't shut up. The evidence was not game time, no one would take the chance on that and, regardless, the history of baseball as talk and traditions would always, like most of the abstract, obstructive convictions held up by the pillars and lights of Yankee Stadium, overrule a few lightning tosses in the schoolyard.

Years later Carlos tried to explain it to poets who didn't get sports: the turn was a poetry of motion, re-vamping the laws of American baseball and writing: verse going in reverse: backwards to the target, to be concise, to get his point across, to be clear, why as a foreigner use one word where two or three will do? Fast across the diamond to first base but turning and doing it in reverse. A first lesson in letting difference make you get where you need to go, differently, whether getting to your point or getting to the bag.

The point was this: Sandy's principledness, the Brooklyn Jew fasting and not pitching even in the World Series on Yom Kippur, was the base of another generation's pride, Carlos Rossman's father's thing not Carlos's thing, who never believed ritual starvation could ride the coattails of a pitcher's ethnicity to the mound before sixty thousand people.

The point was this: at the end of the '61 season on the grounds of Yankee Stadium, the players wheeled out from the bullpen a cart with a giant Life Savers Candy carton and as it reached the mound the motor stopped and out of the box popped ace relief pitcher Luis Arroyo, winner of the team's Life Saver award, having saved ace starting pitcher Whitey Ford's ass all season.

Koufax and Arroyo became Carlos's saviors as pitchers, but that was not the point. It was this: Jews lived among Puerto Ricans among Italian Americans among Blacks in Queens, New York, without anyone ever talking about their pitchers' origins—Carlos could morph at any time into Say-Hey Willie or Sandy or Luis—otherwise everyone would have stopped playing and cut off Edward Charles "Whitey" Ford at his balls if his nickname had bothered them. Instead, Carlos ben [בנ] Carlos Rossman heard fans on the street saying in deep relief, "Shit, man, Luis saved Whitey's ass last night," without ever hearing the ironies of the Puerto Rican, well, saving Whitey's ass last night.

For Carlos ben [בנ] Carlos Rossman and the boys to talk in 1961 about model ethnics in the open air would look as ridiculously overthought and futile as Carlos standing on third, the grounder coming at him and he's trying to force the ball into his glove by shouting at it while yelling "Americans are biased against lefties in the infield." He couldn't convince anyone of that, nor that he could play third. In Amerika, to try to be a natural and play by the rules, impossible for Carlos, was equal to showing his friends what they really needed to see: Carlos shutting up and not making the turn, living quietly inside baseball's history, just standing there, in practice, on third, trying to persuade his dead right arm that his left arm didn't know what it was doing.

So Carlos didn't force the issue, wound up like all long lean lefties a naturalized first baseman, an Insider in Amerika playing by the rules. (Years later, Carlos wondered what it meant to be an Insider playing by the rules: how little time it had taken for the robber baron Bernie Madoff to rip off all of Sandy's investments).

But for now, Carlos dreamt he saw himself from above standing on opposite ends of the infield impossibly playing out his father's fable at both ends of the stick, so to speak, with third- and first-world color-coded bats flying over his head and falling all around him. He imagined airing that lightning phantom ball to himself from third to first as it caught his oiled glove just in time to out the base-runner coming toward him.

## Walid's and Berri's Football Fable, or Don't Use That Move Against Me

The News Is Bigger than the Thing Itself.

The Memory Is Bigger than the Thing Itself.

The American vocabulary in an expanding universe—well—expands. There's no way outside it.

When the foreign boys Walid and Berri were growing up in winter in New York, iced tree branches hung over Hoover playground and football was a game, the thing in itself, their friend Manny Ramos would have called it, had he read Kant.

In this game, unlike today when everything is unlike itself, there were no "wide receivers" or "wide outs," only "split ends," since they stood, where else, on the end of the front line, or were "split" there, at the end of the line of scrimmage away from where the guards lined up to protect the quarterback: the guards who said what they meant and meant what they said as they went down in their blocks for the quarterback, their blood absorbed in the furrowed muddy grass.

There was a split end who played for the New York Giants: Del Shofner, who, with thin helmet and lean pads, went deep / was slow /

to catch the ball / but did, could easily have been mistaken in a romantic boy's film universe for a slim friend, a tall hero, a runaway singer, a Del Shannon, say, one could always wonder.

Without knowing the word "native," the boys Walid and Berri (wah wah wah wah) wondered: "What is this native name, Del? Can we be among these Dels in Amerika?"

When in this game, Walid felt and thought, this end went deep, he caught the ball. Today, however, and tomorrow, as the universe expands, as the television universe expands, the vocabulary expands with it. There is no way outside it. The color commentator does not say "he catches it." He does not say "he holds on to it." He says "he secures it. It is a game of ball security." The emphasis is on investment.

And it is no longer "the quarterback" who throws to him, since he is going "vertical" and the ball is coming from someone said to play "the quarterback position." This language, its expanding descriptors—it extends to "the quarterback position"—is a form of elongated instant replay, exaggeration that fills time and space with what passes as the need to know the next step but is really that much more dead weight thrown on as insight on a treadmill.

These days, it's not uncommon to hear the news anchor say about a professional athlete, when there are no superlatives left, "well, he's athletic, naturally athletic, at that," as if before that moment he had been moving chess pieces on the field. But then: it's no longer a game, so whatever he's naturally athletic at must naturally have a bottom line.

What has changed since Walid and Berri went deep in the playground?

The bottom line. The people in the stands have been drained of fun, and Carlos and Berri look at the grounds and wonder: how does the drainage work? What is the bottom line for a soaked hundred-yard field? Amerika, how much business do you want out of a game?

The language of football recruits the tenor of American business practices with the military lumpen vision.

Efficiency, clock management, strategies, motivation, confidence, territory. These days "the real vertical game" is the military fly-over *before* each game.

Carlos and Walid hear rumors: After he played, Del Shofner became an insurance salesman, but it's not true if you research it. Truth is it was his quarterback, Y.A. Tittle, who sold insurance and who was in a famous photo, sunk to his knees on the field, his temples bloodied, eternally dazed, never winning a title. Heroic.

Carlos thinks: Tittle was his daughter's idol, and from that photo she has written a Pindaric victory ode to her father. But Pindar never sold insurance in the agora.

At the time, going deep in his memory, the child Carlos heard white noise surrounding the game, and it is only now, as he eavesdrops on the kids behind the school gates, that he remembers an omen (of what, he wonders, of bottom line calculation?) he heard years ago in the shadows of the trees overhanging Hoover playground: two kids playing dodgeball, and one stares down the other and says: "Hey, that's my move, don't use it against me."

## Pragmatism and Poetry in Straight-Ahead Amerika

About her sons, Carlos ben [בן] Carlos Rossman's mother offered this answer in a high-pitched Leipzig accent: "Two are poets with their heads in the clouds."

"And the third?"

"He's a pilot."

His mother did not mention that the pilot had lymphoma: eight years of his stoicism and good cheer around a disease he contracted in the 1960s courtesy of the United States Air Force, which he never blamed for his sickness, only joining a class-action suit against the government on behalf of the Atomic Veterans, but it was a simple suit, no rancor. For measuring the planes' instruments in flight, and for washing off their radioactive *shmutz* once they landed, under the code name Operation Dominic, a Pacific Island A-bomb ocean test drop, he received fair compensation for his atomic cancer. And he left it at that: no blame, that was the mission then, let's just get the money now.

The publicity photos have him smiling through a white mask like Gomer Pyle, wearing white gloves as he sponged down the planes. Years later, when Carlos told him about the stills, he said "what mask, what gloves," that could be anybody, and then joked that the only (g)love he ever got in the military was a punctured condom.

He underwent multiple bone marrow transplants and radiation therapies, until they lost count, and like the pragmatist pilot he was, he retired at the VA hospital, living off VA health benefits, in Central Florida, cursing out socialism yet living off VA benefits in Central Florida, a Central Socialist Community of Government Veterans' Affairs Men who wanted the socialist government out of their lives while getting VA benefits. These were military men, measuring men, not crude "how big is yours" measuring men, some even gentlemen, certainly never caught with "their heads up in the clouds" men, since they were always looking at the odds, as if the odds were navigable clouds.

His mother knew the odds were not good, but she also knew how great a pilot he was, how proud she was. "That's my pilot!" she proclaimed, always on a mission, although she did not know how much greater a pragmatist he would turn out to be. Once, when they wheeled him in for a transplant, they asked him if he wanted to be kept alive on a respirator "if that was the only option." Mumbling through his oxygen mask, his wife and children around him, he asked, straight-faced, as if making a bargain: "is the government paying for the machine?"

"That fuckin' crazy, what he said," Carlos heard the Haitian nurse say. "That fucked up cold, man."

In the dead ward air, no one heard: "That's my pragmatist!"

## English Only in the Bedroom

*El hermano de Carlos pregunta: como hacen usted dice en in-
glés, ¡hola! viagra o el sexo azulsí?*

*Carlos's brother asks: how do you say in English, hello viagra
or blue sex?*

English is the language of the world economy. Most people
listening would agree with the television ad for the super-
intendent of schools in a borderland Texas municipality:
every child should be able to read and write English. A tru-
ism, to be sure.

When Carlos's brother heard the promo, he thought: so
much depends on the world economy. This was confirmed
by the next commercial on the screen: the face of the strong,
quiet American man who started having issues in the
bedroom and so took what the street kids watching TV
news with their grandpas were calling *those hekka pills*, and
which were flooding the market, so that Carlos's brother,
sitting in a migrant's shack after the day's harvest, studying
by solar-powered light for his ESL class that evening, wondered: who would translate these issues that he might one
day face with the men and women of this country and all
those *hekka* pills they swallowed only to keep up the world
economy in the borderland bedrooms of America?

## Queen for a Day in Today's Amerika

Carlos ben [נ] Carlos Rossman's brother, the ESL-studying migrant sitting in the solar-powered shack, looked across the satellite air waves of a flat-screen machine and saw a smiling American woman invited, the television host told him, onto this particular program to be awarded a prize, which turned out to be money, money she won because she wrote the most moving letter to the show about what had happened to her and her three-year-old child after she met a man who made the baby with her and who said in confidence he would love them forever faithful, even before the child was born he said this to her and promised her his love and then six months after the baby was born he abandoned them after the smiling woman—a dental assistant—came home and found him in her bed with another woman.

On screen, she smiled the whole time and the host of the television show rose to greet her and wanted to know how do you keep on smiling—"I'm amazed how you do it"—and not crying, but with the fingers pinching her brow and her voice sweetly breaking, she said, "Well, I'm positive, I think each day will be good, better than the one before, and when I watch your show at home and I see people dance in the aisles, I dance with them while doing the dishes, I get inspired, I know things will get better, you make me smile."

Inspired by her letter, the host hands her $10,000 wrapped in a rubber band, and the audience applauds.

Of the possible future in which another man abandons her, no one, not host nor crowd nor woman, says a thing.

And Carlos's brother wonders: if this were a more

pointed drama, then one would wonder if this woman and the audience were being bought off for not saying a word.

In Amerika, Carlos's brother wonders, do people clap, stay silent and remain positive because they're waiting for their reward?

## What the Children Witnessed

*Some time in the future, Amerika's children read two stories back to back from the year 2012, this off the computer chips in their fingers (taking off in their own motherships)*

1

A political husband hits his second wife in a room in their home and the image of the blue-black shoulder round is captured on a neighbor's phone. But later, after the incident and in his look of vulnerable confidence in front of the photographers, this detail is not so much forgotten as merely something to appear in evidence in some future court case. For now, the husband comes across Large as a Public Figure who can, well, well up. "He was very emotional," the reporter says, "when he spoke about being forbidden to see his two-year-old son, who had witnessed the assault and had been whisked away."

2

Thousands of miles east, the old football coach accused of molesting boys in a locker room shower takes to the microphone, "emotional," according to the press, as he talks about not being able to see his grandchildren or speak to them on their birthdays, or go outside in peace, given the press, with his dog. "We just want to see Poppy," the grandchildren say, "with his dog."

## 1

Out West, the husband is looking Large, like the honorably elected Tall Sheriff of this Town, which he is. They are now, after charging him, taking away his gun.

After the order of restraint is removed, coming out of jail in front of the microphones, the sheriff says, crying: "I thank the judge for lifting the order and (*weeping*) I can't wait to go home and hug and gobble up my little boy."

*As adults, different children will ask: "When in Amerika did this start, Poppy, this ritually honored public sentimentalism as a form of redemption for your violence."*

# 7

# Just Call Me Al

*We are not a narrow tribe of men, with a bigoted Hebrew national-*
*ity—whose blood has been debased in the attempt to ennoble it, by*
*maintaining an exclusive succession among ourselves. No: our blood*
*is as the flood of the Amazon, made up of a thousand noble currents*
*all pouring into one. We are not a nation, so much as a world; for*
*unless we may claim all the world for our sire, like Melchisedec, we*
*are without father or mother.*

*For who was our father and our mother? Or can we point to*
*any Romulus and Remus for our founders? Our ancestry is lost in the*
*universal paternity; and Caesar and Alfred, St. Paul and Luther,*
*and Homer and Shakespeare are as much ours as Washington, who*
*is as much the world's as our own.*

*—Uncle Hermann of Redburn*

1

Carlos and Ismail paused each time the natives spoke in the
familiar, which in Amerika was each time they spoke. It was
the natural order of their confidence. "Hi." "How are you?"
As if everyone understood the other to be well. A univer-
salist narrative, to be sure, not to be doubted. "Fine."

So it was not surprising and it was no big thing when,
as teenagers, Carlos and Ismail, not wanting to be doubted
and wanting for confidence, mistook this familiarity for
something more meaningful, and so decided to mimic it:
to make a home for the otherwise isolated names of persons
and places they encountered, as if this was their American
mission. To no one was each his own where each was a sign
of the other, where what Carlos and Ismail heard in sequence was, well, alphabet aligned and crazy, starting with
A, because it was in Amerika they found person and place

and their relations in the world. "We are not a narrow tribe of men," Uncle Hermann told them, "so take in the world as you play."

2

Alley Pond Park
Asylum of Credemore
Allie Sherman
Alex Webster
Alex "I am of the six million"
Else's predator Alex
Alice of the Jewish community

Person or place, they all came together one day, one year, as if they were family, on the highway to the Asylum of Credemore, whose "retards," that awkward American word known to be shameful yet said regardless, not only spooked the park thugs who would ridicule them but so too Ismail and Carlos and their friends, Gingi, Mordico, Berri, who called them this word as they confused this place with the more infamous because more televised Willowbrook State Hospital, where that year the city's media lenses focused on the bruises of naked, wheelchair-spoked children whom the cameras tracked crawling through the gutters and roaming in basements deep in water among severed electrical wires strung out along the unswept floors...

No one knew how they got there, how they corresponded, but each person and place had in Carlos's and Ismail's minds a room from which to enter and exit, as in the American Howard Johnson's, as they moved from one room to the other, *as if it were a scene made-up by the mind*, so that

together these things were captured in a dream sequence reserved for creatures who had just arrived, the *arrivants*, Aliens in Amerika.

3

It was 1969 and from *Alley* Pond Park, at one moment, Ismail and Carlos tossed a pigskin under a row of elms and over the highway and then, in another moment, kicked it soccer-style over another row of elms and over the same highway, so in the next room *Allie* Sherman (*came through*) resigned as coach of the Football Giants as his star running back, *Alex* "Red" Webster, took over, only to have the team collapse that season, while the children fell out of their wheelchairs and wept on the unswept floors, the pigskins floating in the winter spoondrift across Ocean Highway and inside the dark courtyard of the Asylum of Credemore.

In still another room, a nurse wheeled out Ismail's Aunt Else, a refugee from Nazi-occupied Belgium now living in Florida, as she sat tubed and dying of lung cancer not so much in the Miami heat but fanned under the air-conditioned vents in her apartment, where her big-shot second husband *Alex, quickening his mission with the Wall Street spirit, with his reddened face* ate steak raw, smoked his Cubans, and stole money from her safe.

How many Evil Alex's like this could there be, Ismail thought, like the one in the next room, Ismail's "survivor" cousin *Alex,* "*Alex* I am of the 6 million and you who are not a Light Unto the Nations should know it," so brother

Gadi called him out, among the culture of Holocaust orphans, each one out-mistrusting the next, coming to the New Land, be it Israel or Amerika, it didn't matter.[7] To become one, Carlos's mother used to say, you had to act the real big shot, out-mistrusting the next one on the bread line (*hugging the earth for fear of being raptured and losing your place on the bread line*), the way, as Carlos's mother remembered, Evil *Alex* acted with Else before they married, telling her he owned a supermarket in Flatbush when it was a half a corner vegetable store on deserted, Polish Henry Street.

## 4

It was this way of tribal survival in this Amerika which moved Carlos to thinking about Ismail's aunt *Alice*, she of the liberally infringed Jewish community of DC or NYC or the State of Oklahoma where she was really from, it didn't matter, since all liberally infringed Alices of Amerika still identified as pro-Israel, believing they could agree with it or not, be pro-life *and* pro-choice, never wanting to look dead-set against it in order to appear worldly, open, as long as it could survive "as is" even if "as is" was dead-set against others whom it walled in and whose land it occupied. "We are not a narrow tribe of men," Uncle Hermann could be heard saying in the background, and as *Alice* felt this to be true Carlos felt the deep irony which undercut it and which unfolded one evening after supper, when *Alice* sat down in the Amer-

7. Carlos had heard Christian Patty's orphan theory explaining why Israeli Jews seemed to be always looking out for number one, watching their backs. But Carlos didn't believe it. If her theory was correct, he told her, and the Holocaust Jews who had arrived in the land without their parents then bred children who inherited their push-to-the-front-of-the-bread-line psyche, then it only figured that Muslims in Israel were compassionate, generous, merciful, and always watching the backs of others if, that is, they had inherited the traits of their Prophet Mohammed, a sixth-century orphan.

ican suburbs with her converted-to-Islam niece, who asked her: "Mother, what is Judaism? In what do you believe?"

*Alice* stopped, a bit startled, but regaining her confidence, said:

"This is what's so wonderful about Judaism. We are flexible in our beliefs. There are different kinds of Jews. We are not fixed in our beliefs—this is how we have arrived in different lands and survived for 3,000 years," and was disappointed when her once-Jewish niece said: "That's interesting, but in Islam, we like to give our kids a *foundation* in belief," (as the verse "The Faithful are to one another like [parts of] a building—each part strengthening the others," came to her), which her aunt found strange.[8] But why?

Because it was true. To be a Jew was, well, to be an American, one could invent oneself. In Amerika, Carlos thought, you could just call me Al or Alice or Allah, or be cued to the B's, for "Buddha," it didn't matter, you could move yourself from house to house, person to person, belief to belief. If one foundation in God without graven images crumbled, you could erect forbidden idols without a God in another—Jews, for example, *JuBus,* East Coast pilgrims gone West, who had turned to Buddhism for the soul of Judaism. Carlos had often heard "the flexibility" theory bandied about by relatives. It could make them super global Buddhists able to venture outside the ghetto walls, albeit

8. The Faithful are to one another like [parts of] a building—each part strengthening the others. Every Muslim is brother to a Muslim, neither wronging him nor allowing him to be wronged. And if anyone helps his brother in need, God will help him in his own need; and if anyone removes a calamity from [another] Muslim, God will remove from him some of the calamities of the Day of Resurrection; and if anyone shields [another] Muslim from disgrace, God will shield him from disgrace on the Day of Resurrection.

with a stash of mini Buddha statues in their satchels. And venture outside the ghetto walls they did, even as the *Alices* among them clung to the State of the Jews.

But Carlos felt the fear in Alice's response. She was scared for her niece, for whom she thought Islam had become, in a strange twist of historical fate, the very return to what the Jews had ditched in the ghetto when they "bettered" themselves in Amerika. She worried visions of burkahood upon her niece's personhood; "your ancestors came from Posen to Poland to America not to be shot in the ghetto," Carlos remembered his own mother's warning of a different time as he thought about Alice's fear for hers. The ancestors had come to Amerika to leave all that, at least this is what Carlos and Alice had heard from their uncles.

But if Uncle Hermann of Redburn was right and Amerika was not "a narrow tribe of men...," if We [were] not a nation, so much as a world," and if Uncle Leopold of Lahore left the Judaic path for the road to Mecca because it was too tribal, that is, intended for a people of Israel who needed to maintain "an exclusive succession among themselves," then Carlos ben [בן] Carlos Rossman could only guess the great secret no one would confess and which would put an end to Alice's dream and which she never saw coming: that, like a racetrack gambler, she had placed her fear on the wrong horse of a faith, so to speak, with the great secret being only that *the Heart of Islam was American* and that there was nothing to fear.

5

Is this what Uncle Leopold of Lahore meant when he wondered at the start of the last century how the spirit-hungry West could become only more tolerant toward certain other Eastern cultures like Buddhism or Hinduism (think, Carlos thought, how the young self-seekers in the West had always been drawn to the other Hermann's *Siddhartha*), but "Mind you," Uncle Leopold would say, "not toward Islam." The Westerner would never think of replacing these Buddhist or Hindu ideologies with his own (did *JuBus* really surrender their Judaism?), so that as he admitted this impossibility he could "appreciate" them without being threatened by them?

> But when it comes to Islam—which is by no means as alien to Western values as Hindu or Buddhist philosophy—this Western equanimity is almost invariably disturbed by an emotional bias. Is it perhaps, I sometimes wonder, because the values of Islam are close enough to those of the West to constitute a potential challenge to many concepts of spiritual and social life?

Uncle Leopold's question astonished Carlos, who recalled himself, beside himself:

"My name is Carlos ben [בן] Carlos Rossman. I am Puerto Rican and Jewish, I have three-name stature in the Americas, I am the wannabe heir to the American poet William Carlos Williams, who, let's face it, without my name, would be nothing special, would be the same thing over and over again, like a William William Williams, who does not know I am relative to the emigrant Carlo, *a poor and friendless son of earth*, who has, like Uncle Hermann of

Redburn's Amerika, *no sire; and on life's ocean was swept along, as spoon-drift in a gale."*

And Carlos asked: "What on earth was 'spoon-drift in a gale,'" where could it be found? Until he realized it had blown off the water in the air across Ocean Highway and into his eyes and then saw he was drifting on the beach inside its amassing mist and, in a move recalling the words of Uncle Hermann of Redburn, somewhere between a stranger holding a slate which read "Charity thinketh no evil" and the stranger's enemy posting a slate which read "No Trust," Carlos wrote the damp note to himself as if an idea was spinning like a Jinn wheel inside the words, no ideas but in the words: *the Heart of Islam is American*, and, beside himself, wondered how its foundation would be peopled, asking "but who, where drones bury in sand the faithful's houses, where marines piss on Taliban corpses, where Korans are match-lit monthly by the Infidel Occupiers, where villagers are assassinated by lone American soldiers, who, if I post it, if the social media machine tablets take my message for the mass of people peering down at their palms at bus stops when it's not raining, who will believe: *the Heart of Islam is American*, how do I post it when *no one believes in posters anymore*, and who among the Americans, upon receiving the message (and what if they receive it in the rain when for some reason no one ever looks down at their machined palms at bus stops) will have faith in a religion which is so close to them yet threatens them, or, as Hannah once revealed about the Acts of the Founders, will 'plead for some religious sanction at the very moment when they [are] about to emancipate the secular realm fully from the influences of the churches and to separate politics and religion once and for all.'"

He heard himself asking, what would it mean for an idea to be

"so close to the values of the West to constitute a potential challenge to many concepts of spiritual and social life?"

And as Carlos wrote on his virtual slate, *the Heart of Islam is American*, he heard Uncle Hermann in the background:

"Could you now… under such circumstances, by way of experiment, simply have confidence in *me*?" and imagined the American's response:

"I would prefer not to…"

And he recalled Uncle Leopold's words, the convert from Judaism who had become Muhammad Asad on the road to Mecca and who had outlined *The Principles of State and Government in Islam*, so American a document, Carlos thought, but then again so not… and he recalled the words as if Uncle Hermann of Redburn of Amerika and Asad of Mecca were taking turns echoing each other:

"Our [American] ancestry is lost in the universal paternity," Uncle Hermann said.

"The only political ideal which [has] distinguished the Muslims from the rest of mankind [is] the revolutionary concept of a brotherhood of men united not by ties of blood or race but by the consciousness of a common outlook on life and common aspirations," said Asad on *The Road to Mecca*.

"… our [American] blood is as the flood of the Amazon, made up of a thousand noble currents all pouring into one," responded Uncle Hermann in kind.

"Nationalism," signed Asad on *The Road to Mecca*, "in all its forms and disguises runs counter to the fundamental

Islamic principle of the equality of all men and must, therefore, be ruled out as a possible basis of Muslim unity…, that
unity transcending all considerations of race and origin…"

And then, beside himself, like one of the mute human
monuments of that eighteenth-century "orator of mankind"
Anarchasis Cloots, who believed that "Our ambassador ti-
tles are not written on parchment, but on the living hearts
of all men," Carlos the twenty-first-century Cloots-Disciple
stumbled into the Foreigners' Committee as if he were heir
to the vagrants of the world collected by Cloots at the
world's cafés when he was "diving down assiduous-obscure
in the great deep of Paris" in order to make the thought of
*le Genre Humain* a fact on the ground among the stragglers,
the peg-legged Peggy's and Betty's, among the disappeared
ones like Carlos's cousin Karl Rossman, who had applied
for work and stature in K's Amerika and then self-identified
as a lynched "Negro" in Native Jim Thorpe's home in
Prague, Oklahoma, Jimmy the Sac and Fox Nation boy
stripped of his gold medals in 1913, two days after his
wannabe *bubula* cousin K-Czech aborted the scribing of
*Oklahama* in Amerika, among "The whiskered Polacks,
long-flowing turbaned Ishmaelites, astrological Chaldeans,
mute representatives of their tongue-tied, befettered, heavy-
laden Nations," wanting their place in the American Universal Republic, coming to it "like the long-flowing turk"
or like Carlos ben [בן] Carlos Rossman himself with his "imperfect knowledge of the native dialect, his words like spilt
water; the thought he had in him remain[ing] conjectural
to this day," so that he ceased making a sound in an Amerika
which had always been a rhetoric of riches beyond him,
which gagged him as a child when he lugged his green base-

ball bat through the tunnels of what his father called in conversation "*the* Yankee stadium," somewhat the way the natives would enter into a discussion of "*the* Constitution," not because he knew of its historic uniqueness but because he had heard the public address announcer, Bob Sheppard, call out players in the same, isolating way—"Now batting for the Yankees, *the* center fielder, No. 7, Mickey Mantle," so why not call the player out in the Yankee stadium, as if together in *the* stadium they could be in *the* Republic for which it stands, Carlos's father thought, and then, eyeing his son, who was befuddled with *the* hot dog in one small hand, told him to put the other over his heart as they both sang something to *the* one nation under God, "you must sing something to *the* one nation under God now," his father said as the band played, and Carlos wondered but said nothing. What was the significance of the hand over the heart versus the mute hand salute to the temple, which he had seen focused uniformed men perform around the Kennedy coffins on the television? Why one and not the other before the players took the field? Did Bob Sheppard know, did his father know, did anyone know the American history Uncle Eugen would later pass down to Carlos, "that a dead silence prevailed when the word 'nation' was first adopted by Congress. The British nation could as little be replaced by an American 'nation' as the king could be replaced by Congress." And in contrast to how Carlos's father had never heard the word "happiness" in Europe, so that Hannah had to claim it as a fable in Amerika, the word "Nation," so Uncle Eugen had told Carlos, was heard everywhere yet "was one of those artificial words of European coinage that swam on the surface of America's political talk," as if no one really believed in it, like a conviction too abstract to speak, as if it only stood in for the Republic it used to be.

And what could it become out of what it used to be, Carlos—and Hannah, writing missives home—wondered and murmured in his mute eloquence, in his wonderful blind American worship: could the American republic increase, augment its foundation? It was what Hannah in her letters called the problem of beginning, the coming out of nowhere in a specific time at the same time as one was being *bound* back to one's beginnings, *religare*, religion, as in the foundation of the Republic, "an unconnected new event breaking into the continuous sequence of historical time," and Carlos wondered, where *the Heart of Islam is American*, could this be where "the unconnected new event" might begin a principle entirely new but present at the Republic's beginning? This was what was present in the act of foundation, he thought, re-found, and which, *in the light of reason*, was binding (*religare*) the American Founders and the Islamists: and Carlos recalled their words as if Hannah had taken over from Aunt Alice and now spoke with Uncle Asad on the Road to Mecca, taking turns echoing each other, as if they came from the same beginning, the same principle (*principium*):

"It was not just reason," Hannah said, "which Jefferson promoted to the rank of the 'higher law' which would bestow validity on both the new law of the land and the old laws of morality; it was divinely informed reason, 'the light of reason,' as the age liked to call it, and its truths [We hold them to be self-evident, which paradoxically made them not subject to reason] also enlightened the conscience of men so that they would be receptive to an inner voice which still was the voice of God, and would reply, I will, whenever the voice of conscience told them, Thou shall, and, more important, Thou shalt not." (Arendt, *On Revolution*)

And Uncle Asad responded in kind:

"Say [O Prophet]: 'This is my way: Resting upon conscious insight accessible to reason (*'ala basirah*), I am calling you all unto God—I and they who follow me'" (*surah* 12:108): a statement which circumscribes to perfection the Qur'anic approach to all questions of faith, ethics, and morality, and is echoed many times in expressions like 'so that you might use your reason' (*la 'allakum ta'qilun*) or 'will you not, then, use your reason?'"

And Carlos heard himself asking:

"Could you now… under such circumstances, by way of experiment, simply have confidence in *the Founders' Islamist use of reason*?"

And Hannah remembered Asad on the Road to Mecca, signing the declaration as if he were singing it:

> The Right-Guided Caliphate was a most glorious beginning of Islamic statecraft, never excelled, or even continued, in all the centuries that followed it…: To stop at that first, splendid experiment…would not be an act of true piety; it would be rather, a betrayal of the Companions' creative endeavor. They were pioneers and pathfinders, and if we truly wish to emulate them, we must take up their unfinished work and continue it in the same creative spirit. For did not the Prophet say, 'My Companions are a trust committed to my community?'

And Carlos thought: If "My Companions are a trust committed to my community," who are my Muslim Companions?

Are they like the Founders whose "unfinished work" we must take up and augment, while he was still standing somewhere near the mothership cross-writing and erasing his slate, somewhere in his mind between wanting to post the words "Charity thinketh no evil" and witnessing among the population the signs of "No Trust."

Carlos never imagined this as he sat with his father in the third tier of the stadium. He did not even know it was the first park in baseball history to be no park, no field, to be *between the no-longer and the not-yet*, augmented, a stadium following the Greek *stadia*, and the fat guy behind him breathed Cubans down Carlos's neck, all fat guys for Carlos were now Tigers' fans screaming and breathing white Cubano noise down his neck with the words "come on, Big Ears," referring to Don "Big Ears" Mossi, the Tigers' pitcher, who was facing the Yankees' center fielder, Mickey Mantle, while the Tigers' Al Kaline, resembling in Carlos's mind the youthful end Del Shofner from the New York Football Giants, stood swatting flies in Babe Ruth's spot in right field. Years later, Carlos saw himself in the stands, Mossi facing Mantle, Al Kaline resembling Del Shofner or Del Shannon, you could just call him Al or Del or Allah of the Amerikas, all welcomed, and the boy Carlos coming to the beginning of the land from the outside, from up on top, breathing in smoke, looking down on Monument Park, where the first Yankees were memorialized and enshrined after 1929 in center field.

But was this meant to be the House that Ruth or Cloots built, Carlos wondered, years later. Well, Ruth had more staying power and clout but Cloots, like Carlos the twenty-first-century Cloots-Disciple, had the immigrant vagrant's dream and a green baseball bat to boot to bring with him into "the House." It was something Carlos never wondered about at game time. Was the House meant to be the exclusive ground for Ruthian tribal Yankees' idols or could it sell itself "for all" as if it were the Clootsian Universal Amerikan Republic of non-dualistic Buddhist bobble-heads standing in their oneness for those buried in *the* Monument Park in center field? What could they be out there, these stone legends, on what foundation would Amerika rest, what principle, what beginning, *principium*, would one surrender oneself to, what Companions, was it a self-surrender (*Islam*) to a foundation constantly increased, like a stadium renovated over time, re-constituted on values of distinct eras? "We claim to stand there, *le Genre Humain,* as mute monuments," Anarchasis wrote, where in *the* Monument Park in center field the House that Ruth built could meet the House that Cloots built in a vision which for Carlos ben [בן] Carlos Rossman meant that the Heart of Islam could be American from the start and that like *the* Yankee Stadium and *the* Constitution for which it stood it could be worshipped among all the pilgrims who Aunt Hannah had remarked could be "blind and undiscriminating" because "its origins would not be shrouded in the halo of time" and could be seen from the stands or from wherever they stood when they first arrived on the mothership as the *arrivants,* at any moment seeing across time and space mute statues and upstanding citizens anchored in the harbor of the New-York of the New Land while Aunt Hannah was writing missives home:

"Dear Mothership,

Carlos and I, we are here now a while, and Carlos has discovered the strange possibility that the Americans have the capacity to blindly stumble into a future where they will declare *in the light of reason* that *the Heart of Islam is American*. In fact, he is convinced that they could even trace this apparent sacrilege to the Founders' Declarations. In the meantime, Uncle Hermann has confided in us that our happiness is self-evident and, as such, beyond reason and divinely informed. If we are given freedom of choice, he tells us we may force or not force the smile he calls 'the chosen vehicle of all ambiguities,' as it pleases us. So we smile.

As it is, we are appearing to have our fill of it among the Americans, who can't help but have their fun and say that 'it's all good.' And as it is, we see that there is a *great good fortune* which always smiles upon them *in their blindness* and in their confidence, and that they are often filled with happiness, and that they have this *extraordinary capacity to look upon yesterday with the eyes of centuries to come*."

MAY · 61 ·

Acknowledgments

I would like to thank the editors of the *Massachusetts Review* and the *Brooklyn Rail*, where sections of this MS originally appeared.

I would also like to thank Clockroot editors Pamela Thompson and Hilary Plum for their work in first reading and accepting this MS for publication.

My thanks as well to Pam Fontes-May for her superbly crafted and subtle design of the book.

I am particularly indebted to Hilary Plum, whose meticulous editorial imagination shaped a thorough and clearer vision of what this text is and could be. She has helped me to seamlessly translate for the reader the liminal essence of this un-American/American writing.